Iron Insects Invade Indiana

Here's what readers from around the country are saying about Johnathan Rand's *AMERICAN CHILLERS:*

"Your books are awesome! I have all the AMERICAN CHILLERS and I keep them right by my bed since I read them every week!"

-Tommy W, age 9, Michigan

"I just finished THE MICHIGAN MONSTERS! It was the best book I've ever read!"

-Stacey G., age 9, Florida

"Johnathan Rand's books are my favorite. They're really creepy and scary!"

-Jeremy J., age 9, Illinois

"My whole class loves your books! I have two of them and they are really, really cool."

-Katie R., age 12, California

"I never liked to read before, but now I read all the time! The 'Chillers' series is great!"

-Lauren B., age 10, Ohio

"I love AMERICAN CHILLERS because they are scary, but not too scary, because I don't want to have nightmares."

-Adrian P., age 11, Maine

"I just finished Florida Fog Phantoms. It is a freaky book! I really liked it."

-Daniel R., Michigan

"I read all of the books in the MICHIGAN CHILLERS series, and I just started the AMERICAN CHILLERS series. I really love these books!"

-Andrew K., age 13 Montana

"I have six CHILLERS books, and I have read them all three times! I hope I get more for my birthday. My sister loves them, too."

-Jaquann D., age 10, Illinois

"I just read KREEPY KLOWNS OF KALAMAZOO and it really freaked me out a lot. It was really cool!"

-Devin W., age 8, Texas

"THE MICHIGAN MEGA-MONSTERS was great! I hope you write lots more books!"

-Megan P., age 12, Kentucky

"All of my friends love your books! Will you write a book and put my name in it?"

-Michael L., age 10, Ohio

"These books are the best in the world!"

-Garrett M., age 9, Colorado

"We read your books every night. They are really scary and some of them are funny, too."

-Michael & Kristen K., Michigan

"I read THE MICHIGAN MEGA-MONSTERS in two days, and it was cool! When are you going to write one about Wisconsin?"

-John G., age 12, Wisconsin

"Johnathan Rand is my favorite author!"

-Kelly S., age 8, Michigan

"AMERICAN CHILLERS are great. I got one for Christmas, and I loved it. Now, my sister is reading it. When she's done, I'm going to read it again."

-Joel F., age 13, New York

"I like the CHILLERS books because they are fun to read. They are scary, too."

-Hannah K., age 11, Minnesota

"I read the MEGA-MONSTERS book and I really liked it. Mr. Rand is a great writer."

-Ryan M., age 12, Arizona

"I LOVE AMERICAN CHILLERS!"

-Zachary R., age 8, Indiana

"I read your book to my little sister and she got freaked out. I did, too!"

-Jason J., age 12, Ohio

"These books are my favorite! I love reading them!"

-Sarah N., age 10, New Jersey

"Your books are great. Please write more so I can read them.

-Dylan H., age 7, Tennessee

Look for more'American Chillers' from AudioCraft Publishing, Inc., coming soon! And don't forget to pick up these books in Johnathan Rand's thrilling *'Michigan Chillers'* series:

#1: Mayhem on Mackinac Island
#2: Terror Stalks Traverse City
#3: Poltergeists of Petoskey
#4: Aliens Attack Alpena
#5: Gargoyles of Gaylord
#6: Strange Spirits of St. Ignace
#7: Kreepy Klowns of Kalamazoo
#8: Dinosaurs Destroy Detroit
#9: Sinister Spiders of Saginaw
#10: Mackinaw City Mummies

American Chillers:

#1: The Michigan Mega-Monsters
#2: Ogres of Ohio
#3: Florida Fog Phantoms
#4: New York Ninjas
#5: Terrible Tractors of Texas
#6: Invisible Iguanas of Illinois
#7: Wisconsin Werewolves
#8: Minnesota Mall Mannequins
#9: Iron Insects Invade Indiana

and more coming soon!

AudioCraft Publishing, Inc.
PO Box 281
Topinabee Island, MI 49791

#9: Iron Insects Invade Indiana

Johnathan Rand

An AudioCraft Publishing, Inc. book

This book is a work of fiction. Names, places, characters and incidents are used fictitiously, or are products of the author's very active imagination.

Graphics layout/design consultant: Scott Beard, Straits Area Printing
Honorary graphics consultant: Chuck Beard *(we miss you, Chuck)*
Text Prep: Cindee Rocheleau, Sheri Kelley

Book warehouse and storage facilities provided by Clarence and Dorienne's Storage, Car Rental & Shuttle Service, Topinabee Island, MI
Security provided by Abby and Salty.

paperback edition ISBN 1-893699-48-X
hardcover edition ISBN 1-893699-49-8

Printed in USA

First Printing, April 2003

Iron Insects Invade Indiana

Visit the official 'American Chillers' web site at:

www.americanchillers.com

Featuring excerpts from upcoming stories, interviews, contests, official American Chillers wearables, and *more!* Plus, join the FREE American Chillers fan club!

1

"Gotcha!"

Although I recognized the voice instantly, I was still surprised by the tight hands grasping my waist. I jumped and dropped my water balloon that I had been filling up at the spigot on the outside of our house. It exploded when it hit the grass, spraying cold water all over my bare legs and feet.

I spun.

Just as I expected, there stood Mandy McKinley, my neighbor from across the street. If it had been anyone else that had surprised me like that, I would have been mad. Especially since it had cost me a balloon.

But it was Mandy. One of my very best friends.

"You made me waste a balloon," I said, frowning.

Mandy shrugged and dug into the pocket of her denim cutoffs. She pulled out a handful of balloons.

"Where did you get those?!" I gasped.

"I swiped them from Eddie Finkbinder," she replied with a crafty smirk.

My jaw dropped. Eddie Finkbinder was nothing but a bully. If he knew that Mandy had swiped his balloons, he'd be furious.

"You're kidding!" I exclaimed.

"Nope!" Mandy replied. "He owes them to you, anyway. So it wasn't like I stole them. I just got back the ones that he took from you."

Mandy was right. Last week I had a brand-new bag of balloons that I was going to fill with water. I left them on my porch when I was mowing the back lawn, and Eddie swiped them. I knew he did because I saw him with them a few days later. Plus, he was bragging to all of his friends that he'd taken them.

Problem is, Eddie is in seventh grade. I'm only in fifth, and Eddie is a lot bigger than me. I think just about everyone on our block is afraid of Eddie Finkbinder.

Myself included.

But what was going to happen to Mandy and me later that day would be a lot scarier than Eddie Finkbinder.

In fact, now that I think about it, what was about to happen would scare the daylights out of anyone . . . and it all started with a simple trip to the river.

My name is Travis Kramer, and I live in Elkhart, Indiana. I think Elkhart is one of the coolest places to live on the planet. We live near the St. Joseph River, and there's lots of things to do all year round. Among other things, Elkhart is known as the 'band instrument capital of the world'. As a matter of fact, my dad works at a factory that makes musical instruments.

But in the summertime, my favorite thing to do is go to hang out by the river . . . that is, when I'm not having water balloon fights with my friends.

And that's what Mandy and I had planned for this particular day. The sun was out, the temperature was warm, and it would be a perfect afternoon for swimming, Frisbee, and just plain having fun in the water.

We rode our bikes to a park by the St. Joseph River. It's not very far from where we live. Lots of other people go there, too, especially on the really hot days.

When we got there, I spread out my blanket on the grass, and Mandy spread hers out next to mine.

"Want to catch frogs?" I asked her.

She shook her head. "Nah. I'm going to swim for a while."

And with that she jumped up, kicked off her sandals, and ran through the hot sand. She plunged head first into the cool, blue water.

I took off my sneakers and walked down to the shore. There were a few other people milling about in the water and along the shore. Mostly little kids with their parents.

I walked along the shoreline. Not far away,

the swimming area ends and tall cattails grow on the shore and in the water. It's one of the best places I know of to catch frogs.

Sure enough, I spotted one right away. A big, fat leopard frog. Leopard frogs are bright green with black spots . . . that's how they got their name. They're really fast, too . . . but I'm faster.

I froze. Then, I slowly leaned forward, reaching out with my arms. The trick is to move real slow so the frog doesn't know you're going to grab him. When your hand is in reach of the frog—*zappo!* You reach out and catch him.

I was just about to lunge when I felt something on my arm. I barely noticed it at first, but then it felt heavier. I was sure it was some kind of bug, but if I swatted it now, I would scare the frog.

But suddenly it scratched my skin! The bug felt heavy, and I stood straight up and slapped at my arm. I was sure that it was a huge bee or maybe a hornet.

But that's not what it was.

When I smacked it, the insect buzzed off, but it didn't go very far. It landed on a cattail reed only a few feet away.

And I couldn't believe my eyes.

"Holy smokes!" I said quietly.

Right then and there I knew that this wasn't going to be just another day at the park.

2

I forgot all about the frog. What I was looking at made me forget about everything.

The insect—the bug that had landed on my arm—was all shiny and silver. It was kind of big, too . . . about the size of a Matchbox car.

As I watched, it crawled up the stem of the cattail. The insect was so heavy that it bent the stalk. I wasn't sure what kind of insect it was, either. It looked like it might be a locust. But then again, there's no locust I know of that's made of metal!

The creature moved slow and methodical, robot-like, until it reached the top of the cattail. By now the plant was almost completely bent over from the weight of the insect.

Then, without warning, the insect flew. It came right at me and I ducked just as it went by my ear. Its wings drummed the air like a tiny airplane motor. I turned and watched it as it buzzed up into the air, then swooped around and disappeared into the trees.

I stood in the water for a moment, wondering if there might be any more. That was the freakiest thing I'd ever seen! Maybe there really *was* such a thing as insects made out of metal.

Or, maybe it's not metal at all, I thought. *Maybe it just* looked *like metal.*

No. I know what I saw.

A few minutes passed, and I still hadn't spotted any more of the bizarre insects.

I've got to tell Mandy about this, I thought, and I turned around and sloshed through the water back to the swimming area.

Mandy was on her towel. She had her sunglasses on, and she was reading a book.

"You're not going to believe what I saw!" I exclaimed.

"A frog," she said without interest, not

looking up from her book.

"Better!" I said excitedly. I plopped down on my towel.

"Okay," she said, turning a page. "You found a turtle."

"I saw a bug!" I said.

She looked up at me like I was crazy. "So what?" she said.

"Mandy . . . the bug was made out of steel or something! Honest!"

At this, she placed the book in her lap and lowered her sunglasses.

"I think you've been out in the sun too long," she said.

"Mandy, I'm not kidding! It was a real, live insect of some sort . . . only it was made out of metal! It was shiny and silver like a pop can."

Mandy's frown faded.

"You're . . . you're serious?" she asked.

I nodded. "No tricks. I wouldn't have believed it myself if I hadn't seen it."

"Are there any more?" she asked.

"I didn't see any." I turned and pointed. "It was over there, where the swimming area ends.

Over where the cattails grow."

Mandy leapt up. "Let's go see if there are any more!" she exclaimed.

We had just started out across the grass . . . but we didn't get far. The scream of a little girl caused us to stop in our tracks.

"He's going to bite me!" she shrieked. *"He's going to bite me! Help! Help!"*

"It's one of those nasty insects!" I said. "Come on! We've got to help her before it bites her!"

We sprinted across the grass, and we could only hope to get to the little girl before the awful insect stung.

3

Thankfully, the little girl wasn't far away. Her mother was close by, too, and she was there before we were.

"What is it?" the woman exclaimed frantically. With one quick motion, she swept up her frantic daughter in her arms.

Safe with her mom, the little girl turned and pointed.

"Bad!" she said. "Bad, bad!"

We ran up to them.

"What is it?" I asked. My eyes scanned the ground.

"Bad!" the little girl said again, still pointing at the grass.

"Oh, for goodness sake," Mandy whispered in my ear. *"Look, Travis."* She pointed.

On the ground near her towel was a toad.

That's it.

A plain, ordinary toad, no bigger than the palm of my hand.

"Sweetheart," the little girl's mother said, "toads don't bite. Toads are our friends."

"Bad!" the little girl shouted defiantly.

The mother turned to us. "I'm sorry we disturbed you," she said. "But thank you just the same."

"Hey, no problem," I said. "I'm just glad she's all right."

Mandy and I turned and walked back to our blankets. Mandy started snickering.

"I can't believe she was freaked out by a toad," she said. "When I was her age, I was catching them and putting them in a shoe box."

"Me too," I said with a laugh.

We walked across the grass and over to where the marsh begins. We searched and searched, but we didn't see any more of the strange, silvery insects.

"I'm telling you, I know what I saw," I said.

"I believe you, Travis," Mandy said. "I just wish that I could see one, too."

After an hour of looking, we gave up. I was really disappointed, and I was sure that I probably wouldn't ever see another one of those insects again in my life.

Which, of course, wasn't going to be the case . . . because it just so happened that I *would* see another one.

Not only would I *see* it, but I would *catch* it.

And *that's* what got me into serious trouble.

4

A few days went by, and I didn't think too much more about the strange insect at the river. I guess I just figured that it was one of those once-in-a-lifetime opportunities, and I wouldn't get a chance to see one up close again.

Whatever it was.

One afternoon I was in the garage working on my skateboard. It's one that I built from a kit, and it's really cool. I give it a tune-up once in a while to keep the wheel bearings in good shape. It's a fast skateboard, I can tell you that much. My friends will, too.

Suddenly, I heard a strange clapping noise. The clapping sound was really rapid, like—

Wings.

The garage door was open. Dad was at work, so his car was gone.

And while I watched, a large, shiny insect swooped up from the driveway, arced down, and landed in the very spot that Dad parks his car! The creature came to a rest on the cement, and just sat there. Like the insect I had found at the lake, this one, too, was all silvery and shiny, and about the size of a Matchbox car.

I was overcome with excitement. I had given up on ever seeing one of the unusual bugs again, but now there was one in my very own garage!

I didn't move a muscle for fear of scaring him away. So I just stood there, looking at him.

And there was no question what it was, either.

It was a grasshopper.

No doubt about it. I could see his long, bent legs and his two giant eyes.

A silver grasshopper.

And the longer I watched, the more excited I became. The more I realized that no one would believe that I had spotted such an insect unless I could show it to them.

So I began to think of a way to catch the little bugger.

I turned slowly and looked for some sort of container. The only thing that was in reach was an old mayonnaise jar on the workbench. It was filled with nuts and bolts that Dad had been saving.

That would have to work. I leaned over the desk and grasped the jar without taking my eyes away from the shiny insect on the garage floor. I unscrewed the lid. As gently as I could, I emptied the nuts and bolts onto the workbench. They clanked against the glass jar and thumped on the wood, but the grasshopper in the garage didn't seem to care.

Then, with the jar in my left hand and the lid in my right, I began to tiptoe slowly toward the insect.

As I drew nearer, I could feel my heart pounding heavier and heavier. I slowly sank to my knees.

I was only a few feet from the creature, and I could see it really good. It was a grasshopper, all right, but it looked like some sort of machine.

Like it was some kind of mechanical, motorized grasshopper.

Which was impossible, of course—but that's what it looked like.

"Hey there, buddy," I whispered, leaning closer and closer to the insect. *"I'm not going to hurt you. I just need you to hang out for a while so people will believe me."*

I leaned closer still. Sensing my presence, the insect took several small steps backward.

I realized that if I didn't make my move, I risked losing the bug altogether. Catching insects is a lot like catching frogs. If you're not quick, you'll never catch them.

I sprang, snapping the jar out and over the insect. I had to be careful, since the floor of the garage is made of cement, and the jar is glass. If I smacked it down too hard, the glass might crack or break.

But it didn't. And better still—

I caught the grasshopper!

He hopped up and down, up and down, smacking against the glass, and it sounded like a knife tapping a window. The creature must really be made out of some kind of metal!

Very carefully, I lifted the edge of the glass and slid the lid underneath. After a moment of wiggling, I was able to get the lid on. Then I picked it up and screwed it on tight.

And the jar felt heavy! Man! The insect must weigh a pound!

I felt like jumping up and down. I couldn't believe my luck! I had to show Mandy right away.

I hurried out the garage door and down the driveway, stopping only long enough to make sure there were no cars coming. We live in a small subdivision, and not too many cars go by, but you've got to be careful, anyway.

I didn't see any cars . . . but another thing I didn't see was the dark figure hiding in the bushes near Mandy's house—and I didn't even see him until it was too late.

I caught a movement off to the side, just in time to see a water balloon leave the hand of Eddie Finkbinder. Eddie is a pitcher on the school baseball team, and he has a pitching arm that's as fast as a rattlesnake.

I tried to get out of the way of the oncoming projectile, knowing that if I didn't I was in for a good soaker.

And I almost made it.

Almost.

Because the water balloon hit my arm and exploded, spraying me with chilly water.

But that wasn't the worst part.

The jolt had caused me to lose my grip on the jar. Suddenly, it was sent flying into the air, out of my grasp.

Oh no! My jar . . . and my silver grasshopper . . . were going to smash into a million pieces!

5

I heard Eddie laughing as the jar flew up into the air.

"Bullseye!" he shouted.

But I was too worried about breaking the jar and losing my grasshopper to even care what he was saying or doing.

I leapt forward and dove. I knew that my chances of catching the jar in mid-air weren't very good, but I had to try.

I *had* to.

I threw myself forward, arms outstretched like a football player trying to catch a pass. My eyes never left the jar that tumbled through the air. I could still hear Eddie Finkbinder laughing at me, but I didn't pay any attention. I was too focused on the jar.

And at the very last second, I knew I wasn't going to catch it. The jar was just out of reach, just a hair too far to grab onto. I could see the silver grasshopper inside the glass, fluttering around like a mad fishing lure.

I reached, reached, as far as I could—

My fingers touched the jar. I couldn't catch it, but my fingers touching the jar knocked it up into the air just enough to break its fall. The jar hit the grass hard, but it didn't break. My elbows plunged into the grass at the exact same time. It hurt, but I didn't care. I was just glad that the jar hadn't broken.

"Hahaha!" chortled Eddie. "That was a good one, squirrel-breath!" he sneered. Then he lobbed another water balloon.

I was ready this time, and I easily got out of the way of the red blob heading for me.

"I missed on purpose," Eddie claimed.

Oh man, I thought. *I'm in for it now. Eddie is going to squish me like a blueberry.*

But he didn't. Instead, he turned, shook his

head, and walked away. "You're no fun," he said. But I think he only left because he ran out of water balloons.

Whatever the reason, I was glad.

But sadly, I had another problem.

My grasshopper wasn't moving. It was just laying at the bottom of the jar on its side. I was certain that the fall had killed it.

Now I was mad. I was mad and I was sad. I didn't want to hurt it, but now it was too late.

I stared at the creature for a few moments, and decided to show Mandy anyway. Even if the grasshopper wasn't alive, she'd still want to see it.

I walked up to her door and knocked, but no one answered. I knocked again and called out her name.

Still no answer.

Darn, I thought. I was hoping that she would have been home.

I turned around and walked back to my house. It was time for dinner, anyway. At least I would be able to show Mom and Dad what I found. I have an older sister named Lisa, but I'm sure she wouldn't care at all. She hates bugs.

When Dad got home, I showed him my grasshopper. He said he thought it looked really cool, but I don't think he believed me when I told him it had been alive. Mom didn't either. I tried to explain, but they just rolled their eyes.

But I knew Mandy would believe me. She had been with me at the river on the day I had first discovered one of the strange silver insects.

I called her on the phone, but no one answered. The answering machine picked up and I left a message for her to call me in the morning.

I took my jar and placed it on my dresser. Even though the grasshopper was dead, it was still pretty cool looking. When school started back up in the fall, I planned on taking it in for show and tell.

Mandy didn't call me back, and I figured that she'd gone to the movies or something with her mom and dad. I watched television for a while, then read a book in bed until I got tired. I could hear the soft murmur of crickets outside my open window, and I heard a car drive by on the street. My eyes grew heavy.

I fell asleep.

When I awoke in the morning, I knew something was wrong.

I could *feel* it. I just had some kind of creepy feeling that all was not well.

And I was right.

I got out of bed.

Suddenly, I gasped.

Then I gasped again.

The mayonnaise jar on my dresser was still there, but there was a large hole in the lid!

The jar was empty!

I spun, expecting to see the silver grasshopper sitting on the floor. I expected to see him on my chair, maybe, or even on a book shelf. I expected that he'd be right around the room somewhere.

What I didn't expect to see was the dollar-sized hole in my screen. It looked like it had been chewed away by something with razor-sharp teeth.

There was a hole in the jar, a hole in the screen . . . *and my silver grasshopper was nowhere to be found!*

And that was just the beginning of how we discovered that the silver metal insects weren't bugs, after all.

What I didn't know at the time was that there were a lot more . . . thousands more.

They were ugly.

They were dangerous.

And they were about to invade.

6

I didn't waste any more time searching my room. I knew that the grasshopper was gone.

Question was . . . would I be able to find him? It seemed impossible, but I had to at least *look*.

I dressed quickly, left my bedroom and went into the kitchen carrying the mayonnaise jar with the hole in the top.

"Mom! Look!" I exclaimed. "My grasshopper came back to life! He chewed a hole through the lid! A metal lid, too!"

Mom looked at the jar and smiled. "That's nice, dear," she said. "Would you like some cereal?"

She didn't believe me!

"Mom, really!" I pleaded. "I don't know where he went. He even chewed a hole through my window screen!"

"Well, you'd better find that nasty grasshopper and make him fix the screen, hmmm?"

"Mom, I'm serious! I mean—"

"We have corn flakes or Captain Chomps," Mom interrupted. She pulled two boxes of cereal from the cupboard. "Which would you like?"

I knew that it was no use trying to get Mom to believe me. Even if she saw the hole in my window screen, she would probably just think that I did it.

"I'll have the Captain Chomps," I said reluctantly, and I sat down at the table to eat a quick breakfast. I wolfed down an entire bowl in only a few minutes.

While I was eating, the phone rang. Mom answered.

"Oh, hello Mandy," she said. "Yes, he's right here."

She handed me the phone, and I took it into the living room.

"Mandy!" I exclaimed.

"Travis, you're not—"

"Did you get my message last night?" I asked, interrupting her. I didn't mean to cut her off in mid-sentence like that, but I was too excited.

"Yeah," she said. "But we got home too late, and Mom wouldn't let me call you."

"I found a live one! A real, live silver grasshopper! It's real crazy looking! But I lost it. He chewed right through a metal lid, and then chewed a hole in my window screen to get out! I don't know where he went, but I'm going to go look for him."

"You won't have to look far," Mandy said.

"What do you mean?" I asked.

"I mean that I know where your silver grasshopper is. I'm looking at him right now!"

"*What?!?!*" I exclaimed.

"He's sitting on my window sill at this very second! But you'll never guess what else is here!"

"Hang on!" I exclaimed. "I'll be right there!"

"Travis! No! Wait! It might be dangerous—"

I didn't hear what she said. I had already dropped the phone and was out the door, racing across the street to Mandy's house.

And when I saw what was on her window sill, I knew that things in Elkart, Indiana were about to get freaky.

Really freaky.

7

Mandy was waiting at her front door for me.

"Hurry, Trav, hurry!" she shouted. She seemed anxious, and she snapped her head around. Her eyes darted around the yard like she was looking for something.

I bounded across the lawn. Mandy opened up the door and I didn't slow down until I was inside.

"What's the big deal?" I asked.

"Travis . . . have you ever thought that those . . . those *creatures*—whatever they are—might be dangerous?"

"They're bugs!" I said, frowning. "They can't be any more dangerous than any other insect."

"I don't know about that," she said. "And you might think again when you see what I found. Come on."

She led me through the living room and into the kitchen.

"Look out the window," she said.

I did as she asked. A silver grasshopper sat on the picnic table, its body gleaming in the morning sun!

"That's him!" I exclaimed. *"That's the one I caught!"*

Mandy pointed to a place a few feet away from the picnic table. "Now look over there," she said.

At first I didn't see anything. Then I caught a sudden flash of light, like a pinpoint. I squinted. Whatever it was, it was tucked down in the grass and I couldn't see it very well.

"Is it another insect?" I asked.

"Yeah," Mandy replied. "But this one is a little different."

I walked over to the sliding glass door that led to a back porch. "Let's go check it out," I said.

"Be careful," Mandy cautioned. "This isn't

any ordinary insect."

"What do you mean?"

"Wait until you see it," she said.

I slid the glass pane back and stepped out into the sun. The silver grasshopper remained on the picnic table, but the insect in the grass shifted and moved. I'd have to go real slow so I wouldn't scare him away.

Mandy followed right behind me. "Be careful," she reminded me.

When I was only a few feet from the insect in the grass, I stopped.

"Oh, wow!" I whispered. *"It's a beetle."*

"Take a look at its pincers," Mandy said.

I leaned closer and peered into the grass. The beetle was silver and shiny like the grasshopper, only it was a little bit bigger. It had two large pincers extending out in front of it. Each pincer was nearly the size of the insect's body.

But they were more than just pincers. As I looked closer, the claws appeared to be more like saws than anything else.

"That's crazy," I said.

"You think *that's* crazy?" Mandy asked. "Take

a look at what it did to our lawn furniture!"

Mandy pointed to several aluminum chairs near the patio. I turned and stared.

"No way," I whispered in disbelief.

Mandy nodded her head. "I saw it. Mom and Dad had just left for work and I heard a noise. I came out here and watched that beetle do that."

I couldn't believe my eyes.

Several legs of the aluminum chairs had been sawed off! The chairs were useless now, each with legs that were uneven.

"It's . . . it's not possible," I said, shaking my head. And I have to admit that I was a little afraid. Just thinking about a beetle being able to slice through aluminum was a bit frightening.

But it was nothing compared to the wave of fear that swept over me when I heard a sudden whirring noise from the grass.

Because I knew what that sound was.

An electric saw.

I turned just in time to see the beetle take flight—and head right for Mandy and me!

8

I dove to the grass, and Mandy fled. She headed straight for the open sliding glass door.

I leapt to my feet and shot after her. I could still hear the mad whirring sound, and I knew that I was only seconds away from that awful thing landing on my arm or on my back. With pincers that sharp, that silver beetle would be able to—

Don't even think about it, Travis, I ordered myself. *Just get inside the house as fast as you can!*

I ran across the patio, flailing my hand wildly over my head. I figured that if the insect was going to attack me, maybe I could smack him away before he put those razor-sharp claws to use.

"Hurry!" Mandy shouted. *"He's swooping all around you!"*

In two more steps I was at the door, and Mandy was ready. As soon as I was safely in the kitchen, she pushed the glass door closed – and just in the nick of time, too. The flying beetle was right behind me, and it slammed into the glass panel. It sounded like someone threw a large marble at the door! The beetle hit the pane with such force that he actually cracked the glass!

"Oh man!" Mandy gasped. "My dad is going to flip out when he sees that! There's no way he's going to believe that a bug did it!"

"That can't be a bug!" I exclaimed. "There's no way!"

The beetle flew off. Soon he was nothing but a silver dot in the sky, and then he was gone.

"Well, whatever it was, it cracked the glass!" Mandy said. "My dad is going to be furious!"

"Not if we can prove that you didn't do it," I said, shaking my head.

"What do you mean?" Mandy asked.

I pointed to the shiny grasshopper that was still on the picnic table. "If we can catch him again, we can show your dad. Then he'll *have* to believe you."

"But he chewed through a metal lid, Travis! Even if we could catch him, how would we keep him?"

Good question.

"Well, we'll figure that out later. But that beetle was dangerous. We've got to catch that grasshopper so that we have proof. Then people will believe us. Do you have a jar?"

Mandy opened up a cupboard beneath the sink and pulled out a small canning jar.

"This is all we've got," she said.

"That'll have to work," I replied. "Come on. Let's get that grasshopper before he gets away."

We should have known better, but we didn't.

After all . . . we had no way of knowing what was waiting for us in Mandy's backyard at that very moment.

9

I was the first to go back through the sliding glass door. I hesitated for a moment, my eyes scanning the sky.

Suddenly Mandy grabbed me by the shoulder. "Hold on a second," she said. "Close the door."

I slid the glass door closed and Mandy left the kitchen. She returned a moment later with two tennis racquets.

"In case that beetle comes back," she said, waving one of the racquets in the air. She handed one to me.

"Good idea, I said, flipping the racquet over in my hand. I think the beetle would be able to cut through the racquet strings easily, but we might at least be able to keep him away from us.

I picked up the jar in my other hand. Mandy opened the door, and I stepped onto the patio and stopped.

"See anything?" Mandy asked.

I shook my head. "Nothing," I said. "But the grasshopper is still on the picnic table. Come on."

Mandy slipped through the open doorway and slid the glass door closed behind her. We both walked slowly toward the picnic table.

"Stay back," I whispered to Mandy. *"Just in case something happens."*

Mandy stopped. "I'll let you know if I see any more bugs," she said.

I tucked the tennis racquet beneath my arm for a moment to free up my hand so I could unscrew the lid from the canning jar. It was awkward trying to carry the racquet, the lid, and the jar, so I dropped the racquet into the grass.

"Be careful," Mandy said.

"You're always saying that," I said. "Don't worry. I'll be fine."

I leaned forward as I tiptoed through the grass. The closer I got to the picnic table and the grasshopper, the slower I moved. I didn't want to frighten him off.

But maybe he's not afraid of me, I thought. *After all, that beetle wasn't afraid of us at all.*

I reached out toward the picnic table. The grasshopper hunched back a little, but he didn't go anywhere. Once again, I thought about how strange it looked, all shiny and silver. Not anything like the normal brown or green grasshoppers that I see all the time around my house.

I inched forward, preparing to make my move.

Just a few more inches . . . .

Suddenly, Mandy's voice bellowed out in a terrifying scream.

"Travis! Look out!"

I tried to spring and turn around, but I tripped and fell. The jar bounced to the grass.

Out of the corner of my eye I could see something moving. It was up in the sky, but it was easy to see that it was coming for me.

And *fast.*

I tried to roll and get to my feet, but it was too

late. The beetle was much too quick, and as I climbed to my knees the insect attacked . . . and struck me right in the middle of my back!

10

I screamed when the beetle hit my back. I felt an explosive sting, and I knew instantly that I was in a lot of trouble.

But in the next moment, a cold, wet chill avalanched across my entire back. The stinging sensation was gone. My shirt was soaked—not with blood—but with *water!*

Suddenly, I heard laughter—and I knew right away that I'd been had. That laugh was none other than Eddie Finkbinder.

"You jerk!" I heard Mandy shout.

I stood up and looked around. Sure enough, Eddie Finkbinder had been hiding around the corner of Mandy's house.

"Another bullseye!" he shouted with glee. "That makes two days in a row!" He threw his fist up into the air in victory.

As for me, I was sopping wet. What I thought was a giant beetle had actually been a water balloon that Eddie threw at me. The water balloon had caught me square in the back and exploded, leaving my shirt and the back of my jeans soaked.

And I was mad.

So was Mandy.

I clenched my fists.

He's not going to get away with it any more, I thought. *Sure, he's bigger than me, but I'm tired of him picking on me and everyone else.*

I could tell Mandy felt the same way. She stormed off the porch, tennis racquet in her hand. I started walking toward Eddie with Mandy at my side.

We were *not* going to let him get away with this. Not this time.

"Oh, looky, looky," Eddie sneered. "Are the little kids mad? What are you two punks going to do about it?"

You know . . . that was a really good question. I wasn't sure *what* we were going to do about it.

But we had to do *something*.

We stopped when we were a few feet in front of him. Eddie had already picked up another water balloon, and he gently tossed it from one hand to the other in front of him, keeping it close to his body.

"Well?" he said mockingly. "What are you guys going to do?" He pointed to the tennis racquet in Mandy's hand. "Whatcha gonna do? Play a game while we soak you with water?"

"There's two of us and only one of you," Mandy said defiantly. "You're outnumbered."

"Guess again, freckle-face," Eddie said. He nodded. I heard a noise behind us, and then someone snickered. Even before I looked, I knew what I would see.

Eddie's goons.

Sure enough, two of his pals, each of them holding two water balloons, came walking around the other side of the house. They were grinning like mischievous cats.

Great. They were blocking our way back to

the patio. There was no way we could get into Mandy's house and get away from them. It looked like Mandy was going to get drenched, and I was going to get *another* soaker.

But, as fate would have it, we were about to luck out. And it wasn't because of anything that Mandy or I did. Eddie and his buddies were in for a surprise . . . a surprise that started with that now familiar electrical buzzing that came from above.

The sound of a tiny metal saw.

11

"Ready guys?" Eddie asked as his pals drew nearer. They all drew their water balloons back, ready to unleash their fury upon us.

"Oh, I know what you're thinking," Eddie said. He looked at me, then he looked at Mandy. "You don't think that I know you stole my water balloons."

"You took Travis's first!" Mandy fumed. "I was only getting back what belonged to him!"

"Ah, it doesn't matter anyway. I've got enough balloons to soak you guys for the rest of the summer. Okay guys . . . on three. One . . . ."

There was nothing we could do. Sure, we could try to run, but I knew that as soon as we did, Eddie and his goons wouldn't wait until the count of three. They'd just pelt us with the water balloons as soon as we moved.

"Two . . . ."

"Hey," one of the goons behind me said. "What's that?"

Eddie stopped counting. Mandy and I turned.

The goon was looking up into the air, his eyes darting around wildly.

"What's your problem?" Eddie asked.

"I . . . I don't know," he replied. "I thought I heard a bee."

Suddenly, I heard it too. But right away I knew that it was no bee making that sound.

That was that weird silver beetle.

I *knew* it.

I couldn't see where the sound was coming from, but I was certain that we were about to find out.

Suddenly, Eddie swooped down, ducking his head low. He dropped his water balloon and it exploded at his feet.

"Ahhh!" he shrieked. "It's a wasp! A giant one! Ahhhh!"

The next few moments were sheer chaos. Eddie flailed his arms wildly above his head and began running away. His two goons did the same. Both of them dropped their water balloons and they shattered, soaking the grass at our feet.

And in the air, I caught a glimpse of the strange silver beetle again. I was sure it was the same one that we'd seen earlier—the one that had sawed the legs of the aluminum chairs and cracked the sliding glass door.

Eddie's goons took off running, chasing after Eddie. It was kind of funny watching all three of them run like that, their arms spinning madly above their heads.

Problem was, the flying beetle was still around, and I knew that it would be after us next.

"Go!" I shouted to Mandy, and we took off running. I could hear the electric whirring above us, getting closer and closer by the second. Again, I thought of what the little beast had done to the aluminum chairs, and I couldn't bear the thought of what it would do to me or Mandy.

We were almost to the patio. Just a few more steps and we would be safe inside . . . .

But then Mandy fell.

She tripped on the canning jar that I had dropped. Instantly, she was sent flying to the grass, tumbling head over heels. Her tennis racquet fell from her grasp and bounced to the lawn.

And what was worse . . . the silver beetle—that terrible, flying insect with pincers like buzz saws—zeroed in on her. It circled her once, then twice, swooping lower each time. I could see the horror in Mandy's face as she tried to scramble away, but I knew that it was too late.

The silver beetle attacked, dropping out of the sky like a diving eagle.

12

An idea suddenly came to me, and I didn't give it another thought. There was one thing I could try, and if I failed—

No. I couldn't fail. Our very lives depended on it.

In the grass beside me was Mandy's tennis racquet. I picked it up and swung as hard as I could. My intention was to hit the beetle and hopefully knock it away from Mandy . . . at least long enough for us to get inside.

I swung once . . . and missed.

"Travis!" Mandy shrieked. *"Help! Help! It's coming!"*

I caught a shiny glimpse out of the corner of

my eye and swung blindly. I swooped the racquet around as hard as I could.

Bowaarrreeeowww!

I hit it! I hit the beetle!

"Go!" I shouted, helping Mandy to her feet. *"Get inside!"*

Mandy leapt up and bounded across the porch. I was about to follow, but I was too curious. I had to see what had happened to the beetle.

I had swung the racquet at a downward angle, so I was pretty sure that the beetle would have hit the ground. It could have flown off, too. If a metal beetle can crack a plate glass door, I imagined that it could probably survive being hit by a tennis racquet.

But then came a stroke of luck that I hadn't imagined.

The beetle was in the yard! I could see its shiny body reflecting the glare of the sun!

"Travis!" Mandy hollered. *"Get in here! What are you doing?!?"*

Did I dare? Should I try and capture the beetle in the canning jar? If I did, we might be able to find out more about it. We could take it to the nature center. I'm sure somebody there might have some answers.

Besides . . . in all of the chaos and confusion, the grasshopper that was on the picnic table was gone. He probably got scared off.

"Travis!"

"Hang on," I said. "I'll be okay."

I picked up the jar and stuffed the lid in my back pocket. In my left hand I carried the jar, and in my right hand I held the racquet like a sword.

Up ahead in the grass, the shiny object glimmered. It flopped about in the grass.

Man, I hope I'm doing the right thing, I thought.

I approached cautiously, wary that at any moment the little metal monster might take flight and come after me.

Five steps away.

Four . . . .

I could see the beetle clearly now. It wasn't moving.

Three steps . . . .

Two . . . .

I decided not to wait any longer. In one quick

motion I dropped the racquet to the grass, dug the lid from my back pocket, and sprang.

My aim was perfect. Years of catching frogs had taught me how to move quickly, and within a split-second the jar was over the silvery insect.

"Gotcha, you shiny little pest!" I shouted proudly. In seconds, I had slipped the lid over the top of the jar and screwed it on tight. *"Mandy! I've got him! I've got him!"*

Mandy peered out from the partially-open sliding glass door. She wasn't sure if it was really safe to come out or not.

I looked into the jar. The strange beetle was on its side. One of its wings appeared to be broken. It was unfolded from its body and bent. A leg was missing. I wasn't sure, but I was pretty sure that I'd killed it.

And I will say this much: I have never seen any insect like this before in my life. The creature *looked* like an insect . . . but it also looked like a little machine.

Mandy finally decided that it was safe to leave the house. She strode across the patio and over the lawn.

"You really caught it?" she asked.

I nodded. "Yeah!" I replied. "But I think I killed it. It's not moving."

"Yeah, but you said that your grasshopper wasn't moving last night when you went to bed," she said. "And it chewed its way out."

"True," I answered, "but I didn't hit the grasshopper across the yard with a tennis racquet."

"Let me see," she said, and I held up the jar.

And that's when Mandy saw something underneath the wing of the creature.

"Travis! Look!"

There was something written beneath the wing of the beetle!

13

"What's that say?" Mandy asked.

"Huh?" I said. "What's *what* say?"

She raised her hand and pressed the tip of her index finger to the glass. "That! Right there!"

I turned the jar so I could see what she was looking at.

"Whoah!" I exclaimed. "There's something written there!"

"What does it say?" Mandy asked again.

I shook my head. "I can't tell. The letters are too small. Do you have a magnifying glass?"

"Yeah, there's one in the junk drawer in the kitchen. Hang on."

Mandy darted off and returned a moment

later with a magnifying glass. She handed it to me, and I held it up, peering through the lens.

"B . . . T . . . C," I read slowly.

"Huh?" Mandy said. "Let me see." She leaned closer and gazed through the magnifying glass. "BTC," she read out loud. "What's that supposed to mean?"

"Maybe it's the name of the insect," I said.

"Don't be silly," Mandy said. "Insects don't have names."

"Well, maybe this one does," I replied. "It's too bad we didn't catch that grasshopper. We could have looked to see if he had something written on him, too."

"This is just too weird," Mandy said. "This thing had to come from somewhere. If we can find out what 'BTC' means, we'll have our answer."

"Meanwhile, let's see if we can find that grasshopper. He might not have gone too far."

We searched and searched. We started in Mandy's yard, and then we searched the surrounding yards. Then we went back over to my house and looked around over there.

After several hours of searching, we gave up. The grasshopper was gone.

But I was more curious than ever what the letters 'BTC' stood for. I asked my mom, and she didn't know. When my dad came home from work that evening, I showed him the strange insect. He looked at the letters, but he didn't know what they meant, either.

"I really want to know," I told him.

"Hey, don't worry," Dad said. "Wait until you're fifteen years old. Then you'll know *everything.*"

"Really?" I asked, my eyes growing wide.

"Oh, yes," Dad replied, matter-of-factly. "Teenagers know everything."

Fifteen?!?! I thought. *I can't wait that long!*

After dinner, Mandy came over and we made one last search for the grasshopper, but we didn't find it.

Just before dark Mandy looked at her watch.

"I've got to go," she said. "But I'll take a quick look around our yard to see if I can find the grasshopper."

"Call me if you do," I said.

Mandy said she would, then walked across the street to her house. I took one last unfruitful look for the grasshopper before going inside, but I didn't see anything.

An hour later, I was just getting ready for bed. The phone rang. It was Mandy.

"Guess what?" she asked.

"You found the grasshopper?!?!?" I replied. "Really? Did you?"

"Better," Mandy said. *"I found out what the letters 'BTC' mean. You won't believe it when I tell you!"*

14

"Tell me!" I pleaded.

"I asked my dad what 'BTC' stands for, and he knew it right away. 'BTC' stands for *Boogaloo Toy Company.*"

"Boogaloo Toy Company?" I said.

"That's right," Mandy replied. "Dad said that the Boogaloo Toy Company was one of the biggest toy companies in the world."

"Right here in Elkhart?" I asked. I had never heard of the company before.

"Yeah. In fact, the company isn't far from here. They closed a long time ago."

"Why?"

"I don't know," Mandy replied. "But my dad

said that there was something strange that happened. For one, no one was ever allowed in the factory except the workers. *No one.* One day the company told everyone that the factory was closing. Didn't give them a reason or anything. That was that. But guess what the Boogaloo Toy Company was famous for."

"What?" I asked.

"Miniature robots," Mandy said smartly. She placed her hands on her hips. "Dad said that they made miniature robots better than any company in the world."

"But if the company is closed, then where did that beetle come from?"

"I don't know. But I found out one more thing."

"Yeah?"

"I called information . . . you know . . . just to see if there is a telephone number listed for the Boogaloo Toy Company."

"And?"

"There *is!* I called it! No one was there, but I got an answering machine. It said that the Boogaloo Toy Company would be re-opening again very soon."

My mind was spinning. I couldn't believe that the beetle we had killed—or broken, anyway—was a toy. It was too dangerous for someone to play with!

"There's something really fishy going on," I said.

"I think you're right," Mandy agreed. "And I want to know what it is."

"I'll call them in the morning," I said. "Maybe someone will be there during the daytime. What's the number?"

Mandy read it to me and I wrote it down. "But don't you call until I come over," she ordered. "I want to hear what they say."

The next morning, I waited until Mandy came over before I called. When she arrived, I already had the phone in my hand. The beetle still sat in the glass canning jar, and I had taken it out of my bedroom and placed it on the coffee table in the living room. Mandy pointed at it when she came in.

"Glad to see it didn't chew its way out like the grasshopper," she said.

"You and me both," I agreed.

As soon as she sat down in a chair, I dialed the number for the Boogaloo Toy Company. It rang and rang. Then I heard a click, and a woman answered.

"Boogaloo Toy Company . . . may I help you?"

"Um . . . uh, yeah," I stammered. "I . . . I was wondering if you guys were open. My friend and I wanted to see what your company looks like."

"I'm sorry, you've reached our manufacturing facility," the woman said. She sounded annoyed. "This *isn't* a toy store."

"I know . . . I mean . . . well, I heard that you're going to be opening soon. We thought it would be cool to see what your factory looks like."

"The Boogaloo Toy Company will begin manufacturing operations very soon," the woman said. "But we're not open yet. And we never – under any circumstances – allow visitors. Company policy."

"She's really grouchy," I whispered to Mandy.

"I beg your pardon?" the woman on the phone said, and I hoped that she hadn't heard me.

"Have you started . . . um . . . making stuff? Like toy robots?" I asked.

"Don't be silly," the woman said. "I've already told you. We're not open for business."

"Well, my friend and I found this little toy beetle. It's made out of some kind of metal, and it's really heavy. It sawed the legs off an aluminum chair. I hit it with a tennis racket and I think I broke it. It has the letters 'BTC' beneath the wing."

There was silence on the other end of the line. Finally, the woman spoke. She sounded shocked.

"You . . . you have . . . *what?"* she asked.

"A beetle. And I caught a grasshopper two nights ago."

"One moment please." She sounded frantic. There was a click, and then cheesy music began to play.

"What's going on?" Mandy whispered.

"She put me on hold," I replied. *"She sounded really freaked when I told her about the beetle we caught. I think she's going to – "*

The music on the phone suddenly stopped, and the woman's voice came back on the line.

"Young man?" she said.

"Yes?"

"The company president would like to see you and your friend as soon as possible."

Huh? I thought.

"But . . . but you said that you don't allow—"

"The company president would like to see you right away. Please come to the main entrance of the factory. And bring the beetle with you." Then she hung up.

Mandy could tell that something was up by the look on my face.

"What?" she asked. "What's going on?"

I placed the phone in my lap. "The company president wants to see us," I said in disbelief.

Mandy's eyes grew wide, and her jaw fell. "But no one has ever been inside the factory," she said. "No one except the workers a long time ago."

"I know," I replied. I shrugged. "I guess we'll be the first."

In a way, I was kind of excited. I thought it was cool that we had an appointment to meet with the president of the Boogaloo Toy Company.

Maybe he was going to give us a reward for finding the beetle!

Little did we know that we had an appointment, all right. An appointment . . . with *horror.*

An appointment that was only a few hours away.

15

I wanted to head over to the Boogaloo Toy Company right away, but I had some chores to do around the house. Plus, I had to mow the lawn. Then Mom asked if I would walk to the store and get some groceries for her. It was almost one o'clock before I finished.

I carefully packed some newspaper into a small box, then put the metal beetle inside. Then I put the box into my backpack and looped it over the handlebars of my bicycle.

Mandy must have seen me getting my bike ready in the garage, because in less than a minute she had ridden over on her own bike. She stopped in the driveway, pulled a piece of paper from her back pocket, and unfolded it.

"I drew a map," she said, "going by the information I could find in the phone book. The factory is over on Old US-33."

She handed me her map, and I looked at it.

"It doesn't look like it's too far away," I said.

"I think it's about a mile. Maybe a little bit more."

"Let's go," I said.

"Have you got the beetle?" Mandy asked.

I hopped on my bike and patted my backpack that hung in front of my handlebars. "Right here," I said.

We were off.

Twenty minutes later, we stopped at a dirt road that turned off of Old US-33. The road was wide, but overgrown grass drooped along the shoulder. It looked like the road had been abandoned. Far off, in the middle of a field, sat a huge factory. The building looked old and forgotten. A few huge tulip trees were clumped nearby. That's the state tree here in Indiana. Tulip trees can get pretty big . . . a hundred feet high with trunks a few feet in diameter. The ones that grew near the factory were at least that big.

Mandy pulled the map out of her pocket and unfolded it. "I think this is it," she said.

"It sure looks dumpy," I replied.

We sat on our bikes for a moment. I found it hard to believe that this was the place where, at one time, the world's largest manufacturer of toys based its operations.

"Come on," I urged, and I started off. "Might as well go find out."

We pedaled along the dirt road. The old building loomed closer and closer, and I realized that it was even bigger than I'd first imagined.

Finally, we came to a large iron gate. It was closed, blocking our way. And there was a fence on either side of it, too, that stretched through the field, creating a large, protective circle around the factory.

There was no way we were going to get in.

"This can't be it," Mandy said, and she pulled out her map and studied it some more.

"I don't think anyone's been here for years," I said. "Look." I pointed toward the old factory. "There aren't even any cars in the parking lot."

"I must have screwed up," Mandy said. She scratched her head. "But still—"

Mandy was interrupted by loud *clunk!* sound. Then there was a squeak.

The gate was opening!

We stared, our eyes wide, as the gate slowly chugged open. Then it stopped.

"Looks like we've got the right place after all," I whispered. *"Come on."*

As soon as we were past the gate, it began closing. It squeaked loudly, and I couldn't help but think that the noise sounded like laughter. Haunting, wicked laughter. I began to wonder if this was a good idea, after all.

The gate clanged shut.

Good idea or not, we had found the old Boogaloo Toy Company.

And we were about to go inside.

16

About the factory:

It was huge. Rows of windows reached two stories high and stretched on the length of a gymnasium. It was made of brick. I was sure that, at one time, the brick was a bright red, all clean and new. Now the brick had become a dirty, weathered brown. As we rode closer, we could see that all of the windows had been boarded up on the inside.

We stopped when we reached an empty parking lot. There were no cars anywhere.

"This can't be the place," I said.

Mandy pointed. "Look!" she exclaimed.

She was pointing at a pair of closed doors. A

chain looped through the door handles, and a padlock was firmly affixed to the chain. No one was getting inside this place without a key.

But that's not what Mandy was pointing at. She was pointing to an old, faded sign above the door. We were too far away to read it.

I got off my bike and set the kick stand. Mandy did the same. Then I unhooked my backpack from the handlebars and looped the sack over my shoulder. Side by side, we walked cautiously toward the old factory.

A warm wind tossed my hair. It whispered into my ears, and I could almost hear it. It sounded like it was speaking to me.

"Staaaaaaaay . . . awaaaaaaayyy," the wind seemed to say. *"Staaaaaaay . . . awaaaaaaayyyy . . ."*

"Can you hear that?" I asked Mandy.

"Hear what?"

"The wind. Can't you hear it?"

"Yeah, I guess so," she said with a shrug. "Why?"

"Oh, nothing," I said.

Staaaaaaay . . . awaaaaaay.

In one of the tulip trees, a single crow sat

staring at us. Usually crows are noisy, but this one just sat there, scowling at us, like we were trespassing on his property.

Finally we were at the steps of the enormous brick building. I looked up and looked at the sign, and Mandy and I read the words aloud, together.

"Boogaloo Toy Company . . . Keep Out!"

"I think I figured it out," Mandy said. "I'll bet that the Boogaloo Toy Company has built another factory. This place has been abandoned for years. There's no one here."

"I'll bet you're right," I said. "They've probably got a brand new place somewhere else. Come on."

We turned and began to walk back to our bicycles. Suddenly, Mandy grabbed my arm. She stopped.

"Did you hear that?" she asked.

"What?" I replied. "You mean the wind?"

"No," Mandy said. Still holding my arm, she slowly turned around. I turned, too. We stared, our mouths wide.

On the front doors, the chain that had looped through the handles now hung limply. The old padlock had fallen to the cement step.

My heart pounded, and my skin felt hot. A cloud swept over the sun, casting a dark shadow on the building and the field. Without a cackle, the crow took flight from the tree. Soon, it was gone.

And the wind picked up, howling into my ears once again.

Staaaaaaay . . . awaaaaaay . . . .

And while we watched, the two old doors slowly started to swing open . . . *all by themselves.*

17

Mandy was still holding onto my arm, and as the front doors of the old Boogaloo Toy Company began to open, she grasped tighter and tighter. Finally, when the doors were all the way open, she released her grasp. Her arm fell to her side.

"This isn't real," she whispered. *"It can't be."*

"Hello?" I called out. "Is anybody there?"

The wind seemed to answer.

Staaaaaay . . . awaaaaaaay . . . .

I shook my head. The voice of the wind was only my imagination playing tricks on me.

"Hello?" I called out again, only louder this time.

"There's no one around," Mandy said. "Those

doors opened all by themselves."

"Well, it's obvious we're at the right place," I said. "Someone sure wants us to go inside."

Mandy shook her head. She looked at me and pointed at the factory. "Going in there," she said with a shudder, "is the *last* thing I'm going to do. This place is giving me the creeps."

The doors of the factory remained open. There was nothing to see inside except for dark shadows. It sure didn't look very inviting.

"I have an idea," I said. "Let's go back to my house. I'll call the factory and tell them that we can't make it. I'll tell them that I'll mail the broken beetle to them, if they still want it."

"I think that's a good idea," Mandy said.

We turned and walked back to our bicycles. The gravel crunched beneath my feet, and I could hear it speak to me with every step.

Go . . . away. Go . . . away. Go . . . away.

Every step seemed to talk to me. I was glad we were leaving.

I fastened my backpack on my handlebars again and hopped onto my bike. Mandy wasted no time getting onto her bike, and we began pedaling up the long dirt road.

Suddenly, Mandy skidded to a halt.

"Uh-oh," she said. "We've got a problem."

I stopped.

"What?" I asked.

She pointed up ahead. "The gate," she said.

I had forgotten all about it. When we went through the gate on our way in, it closed behind us.

All by itself.

"Well, maybe when we get close to it, it will open again," I said. "Maybe it has one of those motion sensors. We have one of those on the outside of our house. When you get close to it, the porch light turns on automatically."

"I hope you're right," Mandy said.

But I wasn't. We rode up to the gate and waited, but nothing happened.

"Now what?" Mandy said.

"We climb over the gate, that's what," I said. "We'll lift our bikes over, and then climb across. Come on."

I hopped off my bike and pushed it up to the gate, but Mandy didn't follow.

I turned. "Mandy? Come on. Let's get out of here."

But Mandy had a weird look on her face. She was staring up into the sky, looking all around.

"Travis . . . don't you hear that?" she said.

I listened, but I didn't hear anything. Not even the wind.

A moment went by, and then I *did* hear something. Far away, I could hear the sound of a weed-whacker.

"You mean *that?*" I asked, turning to look at Mandy again.

Her face was twisted in horror. Her eyes were wide and glossy, and her mouth was open in a silent scream. Suddenly, she thrust her arm into the air, pointing.

"No!" she shrieked. *"I mean THAT!"*

I turned to see what she was pointing at. Instantly, the blood drained from my face. I gasped, but I couldn't catch my breath. A cold chill swept through my body so quickly that I shivered.

In the distance, in the sky above the field, was a swarm of shiny, silvery insects. Their buzzing grew louder by the second. There were thousands of them, swooping up and down and spinning through the air like flying power saws.

And the swarm was coming right for us!

18

Time seemed to stop. I rubbed my eyes, certain that what I was seeing was some kind of illusion.

But it wasn't.

The swarm of metal insects rose and fell like a boiling cloud, drawing nearer with every passing second.

"Go!" I suddenly shouted. I leapt onto my bike and spun around. Mandy turned her bike around and we pumped furiously, flying along the dirt road, heading back toward the old, decaying factory. My legs were pumping like pistons, forcing the pedals up and down, up and down, trying to pick up speed.

And behind us, the swarm came faster and

faster. I shot a panicked glance over my shoulder, only to see the giant cloud looming in the sky above us. The roar grew louder. It sounded like a billion angry bees.

Up ahead, I could see the doors of the factory. They were still open.

"Inside!" I shouted. *"If we can make it to the factory, we can get inside and close the doors!"*

My legs were quickly growing tired. I can usually ride my bike all day, but at this pace my energy and strength was fading fast.

But I knew that if we slowed down now, it would be all over. Once again I thought about how that beetle had sliced through Mandy's aluminum chairs, and how my grasshopper had chewed through the metal lid of the mayonnaise jar. Just thinking about it made my legs pump harder.

Mandy was by my side, and she, too, was pumping her bicycle pedals like crazy. A rivulet of sweat, a small stream, dripped down the side of her head. For the first time, I realized that I was sweating, too.

Something zinged by my ear, and I ducked.

Out of the corner of my eye I saw a glimmer of silver whiz back up into the sky.

"Faster, Mandy!!" I screamed at the top of my lungs. *"Faster! The insects are attacking!"*

We reached the gravel parking lot. The noise of the assaulting swarm was like a jet engine, and I knew that it was probably directly over us . . . but I wasn't going to risk glancing over my shoulder to be sure.

Another silver insect buzzed by my head, but it didn't hit me.

"We're almost there!" I screamed. *"Ride up to the porch!"*

Mandy was getting tired and she was falling behind.

But we were almost there. In just a few more seconds, we could leap from our bikes and run though the open doors.

Another insect flashed in front of me, and I had to jerk my head to the side to keep it from hitting me in the face. The sudden motion almost caused me to lose my balance.

I made it to the porch and sprang from my bike. I didn't even take the time to set the kick stand. I just let it go, and the bike rolled several feet before toppling over.

I sprang up the porch. We were going to make it.

Or so I thought.

I turned. Mandy had fallen farther behind, but she was almost to the porch. Above us, the swarm of shiny insects was like an enormous ghost, a metallic cloud that churned and boiled. Several insects were leaving the swarm and diving down, swooping in wide arcs and tight loops. One of them spun by Mandy's face. She raised one hand to sweep it away.

And that was all it took.

She was pedaling so furiously and her bike was moving so fast that when she let go of the handlebar, she could no longer control the bike.

She realized her mistake and tried to grab the handlebar, but by then it was too late.

I gasped, because I knew what was going to happen.

In a split-second, Mandy screamed. The handlebars turned, and the wheel slid sideways in the gravel. The bike twisted, and the handlebars snapped violently around.

And as the swarm of metal insects descended from the sky, Mandy wiped out.

19

Things couldn't be any worse.

Mandy was on the ground, and her bike flipped over and crashed to the gravel. A storm of vicious, silvery insects threatened from above, swarming down on their helpless prey.

Without another thought I bounded down the steps. Mandy had already started to get up. Pink patches blotched her elbows where she'd scraped the gravel, but right now, that was the least of her problems.

An insect dove down at her and she swatted it away. "Run!" I shouted as I reached her. I grasped her hand and pulled her to her feet as another insect attacked. This one hit me in the shoulder, but it snared a piece of my T-shirt. Another insect flew in front of Mandy's face, but she was able to duck out of its way.

The cloud was right over us now, and it blotted out the sun. I knew that it would only be a matter of seconds before it would be all over. If the insect cloud descended upon us, there would be no way we would be able to fend off the attacking creatures.

We bounded up the cement steps two at a time. Another insect hit me in the back, but I hardly noticed it.

And suddenly, we were flying through the open doors. Mandy and I each grabbed one, and we pulled them closed. They banged shut, the chains rattling and banging against the metal. A boom of thunder rolled, and I realized that it was the echoing of the slamming door through the old factory.

Outside, we could still hear the roar of the insect cloud, but after a few moments the mechanical whirring sounds faded. From where we were we couldn't see outside, but it sounded like the swarm of insects was moving off.

My chest was heaving, gasping for breath. My heart pounded against my ribs.

"That . . . was . . . too . . . close," Mandy managed to say between gasps for air. "I . . . thought . . . I . . . was . . . a . . . goner."

We stood in silence for a moment. There were several windows that had been boarded up, but beams of light gleamed around the edges, creating a ghostly, rectangular aura. The room we were in was dark and gloomy, but I could make out a desk and some chairs. It looked like we were in some kind of office or waiting room.

But there was no one around.

"Hello?" I said loudly. My voice echoed several times before it faded. "Hello?"

There was no answer. In fact, there were no other sounds at all except for my voice and the beating of my heart.

I walked over to the wall and felt for a light switch. It took me a moment, but I found one. I flicked it up and down, but no lights came on.

"There's something weird going on here," I said.

"You're just *now* figuring that out?" Mandy

said.

"Well, besides everything else," I replied. "I mean, I called and talked to someone here. A woman. But this place doesn't seem to even have electricity or a telephone."

I walked over to one of the boarded up windows and placed my finger between the board and the wall. The board came away easily, and suddenly the room was flooded with light.

"That's better," Mandy said. "Being in the dark was giving me the creeps."

I looked out the window. The sun had reappeared, and the tall, uncut grass swayed gently in the wind.

"Well, it's obvious there's nobody here," I said. "And we only have one choice. Somehow, we have to make it to that fence, throw our bikes over, and get back home without those insects getting us."

Mandy walked to the closed doors and grasped the handle. She shook it.

"And now we have another problem," she said. "The doors are locked."

"What?" I exclaimed. I walked over to the

door, grasped the handle, and tried to push. Then I tried to pull.

It was no use. The doors were locked. We were trapped inside.

"This just gets worse and worse," Mandy said. "First, we're chased by millions of flying metal insects. Then I fall off my bike and scrape my elbows. Now we're locked in an abandoned factory. I mean . . . it can't *get* any worse than this."

Mandy was wrong. Things *could* get worse.

And they were about to.

20

We stood by the door, wondering what we could do. I was thinking that, if we *really* needed to, maybe we could break the window and get out. It would be dangerous, and we'd still have to watch out for the swarm of metal insects, but at least we'd be out of the factory.

"Maybe there's another way out of the factory," Mandy suggested. "I mean . . . there has to be more than just one door. There has to be loading bays where trucks would pull up to."

"Problem is, where are they?" I asked. "This place is so dark we'd probably trip and—"

I had no sooner spoke the words when a light turned on, illuminating a long hallway.

"O-kay," Travis said quietly. "Maybe there is electricity here, after all."

The corridor was narrow, with dirty yellow walls and cobwebs hanging from the ceiling. A few spiders scurried along their webs.

"I'm . . . getting the idea that . . . that someone knows we're here," Mandy stammered.

Mandy was right. The fence outside opened the moment that we approached it. Then it closed behind us, locking us in. Then the doors to the factory opened when we got close, locking themselves when we got inside. Now, a light had come on . . . all by itself.

"Okay," I said. "Let's see what this is all about."

Slowly, we walked through the dark office and into the dimly lit hallway. We had to duck to keep the spider webs out of our hair.

The hall turned, and we followed it. Ahead of us, another light blinked on.

"It's like this place is alive," Mandy whispered. *"It's lighting the way for us."*

We kept walking. The air was dry, and smelled musty and old. I was sure that no one had been through these corridors in years. This hardly looked like a factory that was going to be opening soon.

The hall made yet another turn, and another light blinked on. I turned and glanced behind me and noticed that the light behind us had flickered out.

Man, I hope we know what we're doing, I thought. *We could get lost in this place real easy.*

"This place is even bigger than it looks," Mandy said as we rounded yet another corner.

"Not anymore," I said, pointing ahead of us. "End of the line."

Ahead of us, the hallway simply stopped. There were several closed doors along the wall, but we'd seen a few of them already. I checked a few of them; all were locked.

"Wait a minute," Mandy said. "This one here isn't a door. It looks like it's an old elevator."

Sure enough, the door had a single, vertical crease in the middle, just like the doors of an elevator. On the wall was a panel. I looked closer. There were only two buttons on the panel. One of them had an arrow pointing up, and the other had an arrow pointing down.

"You're right!" I said. "It *is* an elevator!"

As soon as I uttered those words, the elevator doors swept open. Light burst forth. It happened so quickly that Mandy and I jumped and retreated, our backs against the far wall.

In front of us, the elevator doors remained patiently open. A yellow light glowed eerily from inside the tiny room.

"I guess we're going for a ride," I whispered. "Come on."

I stepped forward, hesitated an instant, then stepped into the elevator. I bounced up and down a little to make sure the elevator was safe. It looked like it hadn't been used in a hundred years.

Mandy was still backed up against the wall on the other side of the hall. She had a look of uncertainty on her face.

"Come on," I said. "It'll be okay."

Reluctantly, Mandy stepped forward, pausing at the door. Then she stepped inside.

Instantly, the door slid closed. We both jumped in surprise.

We waited, but nothing happened. On the wall was a small panel. There were two buttons. One was labeled G, the other was labeled 2.

"Might as well see what's on the 2nd floor," I said, and I reached out and pressed the button labeled 2.

Nothing happened.

I pressed it again, and then inspected the layer of dust on my finger that had come off when I pressed the button. No one had used this elevator in a long time.

Suddenly, there was a loud clunk, and the whir of a motor. The elevator began to tremble and shake.

"Maybe this wasn't a good idea," I said, and I reached out quickly and tried to pry the doors open. They wouldn't budge.

All of a sudden the elevator began to move. It started slowly, but then it began picking up speed.

But something was very, very wrong.

"Travis!" Mandy exclaimed in horror. *"How can this be?!?!"*

"I don't know!" I answered, fear simmering in my voice. "It's . . . it's impossible! We were already on the ground floor!"

The elevator was moving, all right. But we weren't going up . . . we were going *down*.

And *fast!*

21

However crazy it sounded, we weren't going up.

We were going down. We were going down, and our speed was increasing with every passing second.

"This is crazy!" I said. "How can this be! It's like we're going into the ground!"

Mandy didn't say a thing. She had backed up to the wall of the elevator, her hands pressed against the cold steel. The elevator was really shaking now, but there was nothing we could hold on to.

All the while, I could feel our speed increasing. We were going faster and faster and faster.

"What if the cables broke!" Mandy cried. "What if they broke . . . and we go all the way to the bottom of the elevator shaft!?!?"

That's not something that I wanted to think about, but it was a real possibility. The elevator *was* very old. If, for whatever reason, the elevator shaft had been built deep into the ground, and if the cables had broken, we'd be crushed at the bottom by sheer force.

I pressed the buttons frantically, trying to do anything I could to slow down our rapid descent, but nothing worked.

The light above us blinked on and off. A single bell chimed.

And the elevator began to slow.

The quaking and trembling eased.

The elevator slowed even more, and it was a weird feeling. It felt like I was really heavy. My legs had a hard time supporting the rest of my body, because the downward force pressed upon me from the rapid decrease in our descent.

Then, ever so slowly, the elevator crept to a stop. A single bell chimed. Again, I could hear the pounding of my heart.

But when the door suddenly slid open, I sucked in a gasp of air that ballooned in my lungs. Mandy did, too.

Nothing . . . *nothing* . . . could have prepared us for what we were seeing at that very moment.

22

We were in a factory, all right. A busy factory, filled with churning machines and whirring motors and spinning cables and pulleys. Metal clanged and banged. A conveyer belt whined.

But there wasn't a single person in sight.

Mandy and I stood in the elevator, dumbfounded by the sight before us. The factory that we'd seen in the field—the one that we'd entered—was cold and lifeless, but what we were seeing now was a bustle of activity.

But strangely, there wasn't a single person in sight.

Mandy and I were still standing in the elevator, and I was the first to take a guarded step through the door. Mandy followed, and as soon as we were both outside, the elevator doors slid closed.

"Where . . . where in the world are we?" Mandy stammered.

I turned my head slowly and gazed at all the machinery.

"Well, we're in some factory, that's for sure," I replied. "This must be a secret underground plant or something."

We stood in front of the elevator, uncertain of what to do or where to go. It seemed strange that all of this equipment was operating without any workers around. All of the machines and gadgetry seemed to be working under its own power.

"Maybe we shouldn't be here," Mandy said. "Maybe we went the wrong way on that elevator.

I shook my head. "I tried to push the buttons to go up," I said, "but we came down here anyway."

"Do you think this might be the Boogaloo Toy Company?" Mandy asked.

Again, I shook my head. "I don't know," was

all I said.

While we were standing there, looking around, I heard another sound. Mandy did, too. It was a motorized, buzzing sound that didn't seem to be coming from any of the machines or equipment.

And it sounded like it was coming closer.

Suddenly, Mandy's arm shot out.

"Travis! Look!"

Something moved in an aisle between several machines, but I couldn't tell what it was. It didn't seem to be very big . . . perhaps about as big as a medium-sized dog. And whatever it was, it was making a buzzing, machine-like noise.

Mandy inched closer and squeezed my hand.

"Don't worry," I said to her, trying to be brave. "We'll be fine."

Then, in the blink of an eye, the thing that had moved showed itself by lunging into the open—and I wasn't so sure that we were going to be fine.

Mandy screamed and turned to flee back into the elevator, but the doors had closed and she couldn't get them open. As for me, I backed up to the doors of the elevator, but my eyes stayed focused on the strange thing I was seeing.

It was an *insect.* An insect made of metal. It looked like a giant locust made of steel, and it moved like a robot. Its eyes were silver and shiny, and its legs . . . all six of them . . . were long and wiry.

The strange creature remained on the floor for a moment, turned its head around, then turned back to face us.

And when the hideous metal beast attacked, there was nowhere we could go.

23

The terrifying creature attacked so fast that we couldn't have escaped if we tried. I couldn't believe how fast the thing moved. It scrambled across the floor with lightning speed, but it stopped right in front of us.

Mandy and I were backed against the closed doors of the elevator. Even if we tried to run, we didn't know our way around this place. Besides . . . if there was one of these little beasts running around, there might be more.

The giant metal insect remained at our feet, staring up at us. It had two metal antennae, and they swished about like thin, wiry cords.

Then I had an idea.

I wasn't sure what the creature was up to, but it sure looked dangerous. While I still had the chance, I decided that I would try and kick the thing as hard as I could. That would allow me and Mandy to run. Where we would go I hadn't a clue . . . but I couldn't just stand here and wait for this metal monster to take a chunk out of my leg!

"Get ready to run, Mandy," I whispered.

"O . . . okay," she peeped.

I was just about ready to kick the creature to smithereens when I was stopped by a voice—and a movement from behind one of the machines.

Suddenly, a man came into view! He had gray hair, a gray beard and glasses with lenses so thick that it made his eyes look like giant brown ping-pong balls. A grease-stained smock hung down to his knees, and his pants were a charcoal-blue color. His shoes were black and looked very worn.

"So! What do you think?" he asked.

I was too stunned . . . and still too terrified to move. The man didn't look like he was going to hurt us, but then again, I couldn't be too sure.

The man began walking toward us, and now I could see that he was carrying a small box in his hands.

"You think that is impressive?" he said with a smile. "That's nothing! Watch this!"

He made some adjustments to the box, and suddenly the insect on the floor in front of us spread its wings.

"Yes, yes, here we go," the man said, and Mandy and I watched in amazement as the gigantic metal insect before us suddenly took flight! The robot-like machine buzzed up into the air and circled around. Then, as the man made another adjustment on the box, the insect did a full loop-de-loop, circled one more time, then hovered in place.

"And watch this," the man said. He made another adjustment to the box in his hand, and the flying creature buzzed high into the air. Its metal wings whipped the air furiously as it rose higher and higher.

The man's head was tilted back, staring up at the buzzing insect.

"Here we go," he said. "Watch!"

Suddenly, the giant insect dipped and quickly began to come down.

The problem was, it was headed right for me and Mandy!

24

Mandy shrieked, and I screamed. The silver insect came right at us so fast that I just knew we were being attacked.

"Watch out!" the old man shouted. *"Get out of the way!"*

Without another second of hesitation, Mandy and I dove to the side—and just in time, too. As I hit the floor, I heard a crash. I rolled sideways just in time to see the insect slam into the closed elevator doors. It slid to the floor in a clump of twisted metal. Its legs and antennae were bent, and it was making a weird ticking sound. Smoke was rolling out from beneath its wings.

"Sorry about that," the man said as he

approached us. I got to my feet, and so did Mandy. The man walked right past us and kneeled down, looking at the smashed insect.

"I've got a little work to do on this one, I guess," he said.

"Who are you? And where are we?" I asked.

The man looked at me like I was a space alien. Actually, with his glasses on, it was *he* who looked like the space alien. Behind the thick lenses his eyes looked enormous.

"Why, you know quite well where you are," he replied. He waved his arm around and gestured to the equipment in the large room. "You are in the Boogaloo Toy Factory. I am Oliver Buggs, president. I was the one who summoned you."

"But . . . but I talked to a woman," I replied.

At this, his eyes grew even wider as he raised his eyebrows. "Ah, yes, my assistant. Katy! Please come here and meet our guests!"

There was a shuffling sound, and then another motorized buzzing . . . and then Katy came into view.

"She's . . . she's a robot?" I said in a voice just

louder than a whisper.

"Oh, quite so," Oliver Buggs replied. "But really, she's much more than that.

'Katy' was a machine. She was a robot that was about as tall as me. She had the dimensions and size of a human, but her legs didn't move. She just sort of rolled toward us. Her arms remained stiff and motionless.

"Welcome to the Boogaloo Toy Company," she said, in a perfectly human voice. It was the same voice that I'd heard on the phone!

"Allow me to introduce my assistant, Miss Katy Didd," Oliver Buggs said. "Katy has been with the company since I invented her over ten years ago."

"You mean . . . you *built* her?" Mandy asked.

"Precisely," the man said. "And I couldn't get by without her. Katy is a very big help. Thank you Katy."

"You're welcome, Mr. Buggs," Katy the robot replied. And with that, she turned and rolled off.

"Is that what you make?" I asked. "Robots?"

"Yes!" Mr. Buggs replied. "All kinds. Remote control robots, even robots that can actually 'think' . . . like Katy. Quite exceptional, don't you think?"

"Well, yes and no," I said. "We were attacked by a bunch of your insects a little while ago."

Mr. Buggs shook his head. "No, I'm afraid you weren't. *My* insects would never do such a thing."

"Yes they would," Mandy insisted angrily, "and they did!"

"What I mean, young lady, is that *I* was not the one that made those insects. You were attacked, yes, but I had nothing to do with it. By the way . . . where is the one you found?"

"It's still in my backpack," I said. "I had to leave it on the ground where it fell. I'm sorry I wasn't able to bring it, but we were being attacked."

Mr. Buggs frowned and stroked his beard. "Hmmmm," he said. "Well. No matter. I guess I don't need it. I just wanted to see what his robots looked like. A few of them must have malfunctioned and strayed from the swarm."

"So . . . if you didn't make the insects that attacked us . . . then who did?" I asked.

Mr. Buggs looked at me, and then looked at Mandy.

"I suppose you need to know," he began, "especially since there is a good chance that the entire city of Elkhart will soon be under attack."

The entire city of Elkhart?!?!? Oh no!

25

"This will be easier to explain if you both come to my office. Please."

Mr. Buggs turned and began to walk away. I looked at Mandy and she looked at me. I raised my eyebrows as if to say *'might as well'*, and we both followed Mr. Buggs.

The factory was even bigger than I thought. As we wove in and around giant machines and mechanical apparatus, Mr. Buggs explained to us about the Boogaloo Toy Company.

"I started the company many years ago," he said, waving his hand in a wide, slow sweep. "Of course, our factory wasn't *here*. It was above ground, in the building you entered. By the way, it was I who opened the gate and the door. I'm sure you were wondering about that. I have cameras built in so I can see if anyone is coming. I can open locks and doors, turn on lights . . . all by remote control."

We walked around a large machine with a conveyer belt running along side of it. On the belt were small parts that looked like insect legs.

"Then why did you ask us to come if you knew we were going to be attacked by those insects?" Mandy asked.

"That is something I didn't know," he replied. "In fact, I don't know how *he* knew."

"Who's 'he'?" I asked.

"I'll explain in a moment. Ah! Here we are. My office." He walked through a door and turned on a light. "Please. Come in, children."

I gasped, and I heard Mandy gasp behind me.

In Mr. Buggs's office were hundreds – maybe *thousands* – of silver insects. They clung to the walls, they sat on desks and chairs. Some were even suspended from the ceiling with thin wires.

Sensing our fear, Mr. Buggs turned to us. "Oh, don't worry," he said. "They aren't alive. In fact, none of these even have batteries yet."

"Metal insects," I said in wonder.

"Ah! But better!" he exclaimed. "*Iron* insects. Much better than mere metal. The iron I make here is very strong. My insects are built to last and last and last. That is why he wanted them so badly. Because they are the best."

"But who is 'he'?" I asked again.

"He's a thief, that's who he is," Mr. Buggs said with a scowl. "Years ago, when I built the company, I hired several hundred workers to help. We built a fine company, with good workers and great toys. In fact," he continued proudly, "the Boogaloo Toy Company was once the world's largest manufacturer of robotic toys."

"Then why did you go out of business?" Mandy asked. "Why did you fire everybody?"

"I discovered that someone who worked here was stealing my secrets," Mr. Buggs replied. "There was someone in the factory who was swiping my ideas and all of my plans, with the hopes of making their own robotic toy company. I didn't know who it was, and I had no choice but to let all of the workers go. I was fortunate enough to find this place . . . an abandoned mine . . . to continue my operations. You see, I was working on a top-secret toy. A toy that children would love and would have a great deal of fun with."

Mr. Buggs turned and picked up an iron insect that looked like it might be an oversized June bug.

"My crowning achievement," he said, holding the shiny insect up. "Remote controlled insects. They crawl, they fly, and they'll last forever."

"But who would steal your idea?" I asked.

"Yeah," Mandy chimed in. "And why?"

"Someone who is very crafty," Mr. Buggs scowled. "Someone who was jealous of my talents. Someone who is greedy and wants to use my iron insects to gain wealth and power."

"One of your workers?" I asked. "Someone who worked for you?"

"Someone I trusted," Mr. Buggs said. "Someone I would have never expected. That someone . . . is my very own brother, Harry Buggs."

Mandy and I didn't say a word. We couldn't. We were both speechless.

"My brother Harry," Mr. Buggs continued, "has stolen the plans for my insects, and he is now making his own. He has used a computer to program them to do what he wants them to do. What I invented were remote control toys for children to enjoy. What my brother is making are tiny iron beasts that he wants to use to gain power. First he'll start with Elkhart. My brother will program the insects to attack the innocent people in the city. People won't even be able to go outdoors for fear of being attacked by one of those vicious little beasts."

"Then he'll use them to attack other cities?" I asked.

Mr. Buggs shrugged. "Who knows? My brother is mad. He's crazy. He's even making his own insects and putting the initials of the Boogaloo Toy Company on them, so that if his plan is discovered, people will think that *my* company is responsible! He'd do anything to get what he wants. But we can stop him."

"We?" Mandy asked. "You mean . . . like *us?*"

Mr. Buggs nodded. "Yes. We. You two, and I, can stop him. It will be dangerous, yes. But we can stop him."

"You're asking us to be—like—bug killers?" Mandy asked.

"I'm asking you to help save the city before it's too late," Mr. Buggs replied.

"Tell me what we have to do, first," I said.

But when Mr. Buggs shared his plan, I knew that it would fail. If what he had told us about his brother and the iron insect invasion, there would be no one who could stop them.

Not even us.

26

Oliver Buggs told us the only way to stop the iron insects was by re-programming the giant computer in his brother's factory.

"But I don't know anything about computer programming," I said. "I built my own website, but that's a lot different."

"You won't have to," Mr. Buggs explained. He reached into his pocket and pulled out a gray computer diskette. "This diskette contains a computer code that will reprogram his system. It will automatically re-configure the entire mainframe, and Harry will no longer have control over the insects. In fact, it will also allow me to use my computer, through a remote radio signal, to control all of the insects. Using my apparatus here, I can command each and every iron insect to fly back to my factory."

"But what about the swarm of insects that attacked us?" I asked. "Where did they come from?"

"Years ago, when my brother began to make his insects, he programmed a swarm of them to surround my factory to make sure that I would never leave. Occasionally, an insect or two will malfunction and get separated from the swarm.

"Like the ones Travis and I found?" Mandy asked.

"Exactly," Mr. Buggs said with a nod.

"You're *trapped* here?" I asked.

Mr. Buggs shook his head. "No. Harry doesn't know that I have an underground escape route—a tunnel—that I use to come and go. I need to go to the store for food, you know. Harry knows that I'm getting out of the factory somehow, he just doesn't know *how*."

"So you want us to sneak into your brother's factory and put the diskette into his computer?" Mandy asked.

"Exactly," Mr. Buggs replied. "It won't be easy, and I'm sorry I had to drag you two into this mess. But I need your help. The entire city of Elkhart needs your help."

"What will *you* be doing?" I asked.

"I will give you each a tiny radio. Look."

He opened a drawer and produced two very small objects that were each about half the size of a dime.

"This will clip on behind your ears. When you wear them, they will act just like a radio. I will be able to speak with you, and you can speak with me. You can even speak with each other, if you get separated."

"Cool!" I said. "Are you going to sell those in toy stores?"

"I'm afraid not," Mr. Buggs said. "I think children would enjoy them, but I'm afraid that they will be misused by others for unscrupulous purposes."

"What does 'unscrupulous' mean?" Mandy asked.

"Crooked or corrupt," Mr. Buggs replied.

"Oh," Mandy said. "And how do we get out

of here? Through the secret tunnel that you use?"

"Precisely," Mr. Buggs replied. "But you'll have to be careful. I know that my brother Harry will have his swarm looking for you. Through his computer monitor in his factory, he can see what the iron insects see."

"I can't believe this is happening," Mandy said. "This is like a science fiction movie."

"Well, it's happening, all right," Mr. Buggs said with a regretful nod. "And we have to stop it. We must stop my brother Harry before it's—"

Mr. Buggs was interrupted by the grinding sound of a loud buzzer. He sat straight up.

"No!" he exclaimed, leaping to his feet. *"It can't be! Not yet!"*

He rushed out of his office. Mandy and I jumped up and followed him to a large computer screen.

"What?" I asked. "What is it?"

"My radio signal tracker has picked up static charges of communication from Harry's computer!" Mr. Buggs explained. "He's already set his plan in motion! Quickly! You must leave and head for his factory!" He turned and ran back into his office, then returned with the computer diskette and the two tiny radios. He clipped one to my ear, and then one to Mandy's. Then he clipped one onto his own ear.

"Come! I'll show you the secret tunnel!"

"But where do we go?!?!" I asked frantically. "What do we do?!?!"

"I can explain while you're on your way!" Mr. Buggs replied. "Follow me!"

He started to run, and Mandy and I followed him. For an old guy, he sure could run fast.

We came to a door in the wall. Mr. Buggs pressed a button and the door slid open. On the other side was a dark tunnel.

"This is an old mine shaft, from years ago when they were looking for gold," Mr. Buggs said.

"There's no gold in Elkhart!" Mandy and I said in unison.

"That's why they're abandoned," Mr. Buggs said. "Here."

He reached over to a machine that was whirring. Next to it was a shelf that held numerous tools and small pieces of machinery.

On a lower shelf was a flashlight, and he snapped it up and handed it to me.

"You'll need this while you're in the tunnel," he said. "It's very, very dark. Now . . . go!"

"But—" I began to protest, but he raised his hand and pointed to his ear.

"Talk to me on the way!" he said urgently. "I'll tell you what you need to do when you're in the tunnel. Go!"

Mandy and I ducked into the tunnel.

"Good luck!" he said, and he closed the door.

We were in total darkness . . . and we were on our own.

27

I clicked the flashlight on and a white cone of light burst forth, illuminating the rock walls around us. I shined the light around.

Suddenly, Mr. Buggs's voice was in my ear! It sounded squeaky and scratchy, but I could hear him good.

"Can you hear me?" he said.

"Yes," Mandy and I said at the same time.

"Good. Get moving along the tunnel. It's very straight, and you won't have any problem following it. There are no side tunnels to get lost in."

We started walking.

"How far does this tunnel go?" I asked.

"Several hundred yards," his voice squawked in my ear. "It's really not very far. You'll emerge on the side of a hill not far from Old US-33. However, I've covered the entrance to the tunnel with branches and brush to keep it hidden. You'll have to move them out of your way to get out."

That sounded simple enough.

"But where do we go once we get out?" Mandy asked.

"You'll head directly to the Noteworthy Horn and Tuba Company," Mr. Buggs replied.

"Say *what?!?!*" I exclaimed.

"That's right," Mr. Buggs said. "That's where my brother has based his operations."

"But they make musical instruments," I said.

"Oh no they don't," Mr. Buggs replied sharply. "He only calls it the Noteworthy Horn and Tuba Company because he doesn't want people to know what he's really doing. He's not making musical instruments—he's making iron insects. *Dangerous* iron insects. In fact, even the people that work for him don't know what he's really making. They all manufacture small parts, but my brother has the insects assembled in his private laboratory."

"So the people that work there actually think that they are making parts for musical instruments?" Mandy asked.

"That's right," Mr. Buggs replied. "They are completely innocent."

We walked quickly through the tunnel without saying much more. I still was trying to put everything together in my head. I knew that Mandy was just as confused as I was.

Finally, we saw a gleam of light up ahead.

"I think we're at the entrance of the tunnel," I said.

"Good!" Mr. Buggs's squawked in my ear. "Do you know how to get to the Noteworthy Horn and Tuba Company?"

"Yeah," I said. "But it's a mile up the road. It's going to take us a few minutes to get there."

"Go as fast as you can," he said. "Leave the flashlight at the entrance of the cave so you don't lose it. You'll need it when you come back this way."

We reached the entrance of the tunnel. I clicked off the flashlight and set it down on the hard ground. Then Mandy and I pulled the branches and brush away from the entrance. In a matter of seconds, there was enough room for us to climb through.

"Ummm . . . Mr. Buggs?" I said quietly."

"Yes, go ahead."

Mandy and I were standing on the side of a small hill. In the distance, we could see the old factory we'd entered. The sun was out, and only a few clouds were scattered across the sky.

"What about those insects that attacked us just a little while ago? Aren't they still around?"

"Yes," Mr. Buggs replied. "But I've jammed the radio frequency that my brother is using to control them. I won't be able to do it for long, though. Once he knows what I'm doing, he'll change to another frequency. You've got to hurry!"

"But how will we get into the factory?" I asked.

"I'll explain soon! Please, children! You must hurry!"

"Come on," I said to Mandy. We both started to run, but not too fast. I didn't want to get worn down and not be able to make it. A mile is a long way to run.

We huffed and puffed along the shoulder of the road. A few cars went by, and I wondered if the drivers or passengers were aware of what might happen, right here in Elkhart, if we didn't stop Harry Buggs in time.

No, probably not, I thought. *Mandy and I are probably the only people in the city that know what could happen.*

"We're almost there," Mandy said.

"Excellent," Mr. Buggs said in our ears. "You'll need to—"

He stopped speaking, and for a moment I thought that my radio had broken.

"Mr. Buggs?" I said.

"We've got trouble," he replied. "My brother Harry has changed radio frequencies. I've lost control of the swarm!"

Those were not the words I wanted to hear.

And when I looked over my shoulder behind me, I saw a sight that I definitely did *not* want to see.

A swarm of thousands of iron insects!

28

The swarm rose high in the air, shining like an aluminum cloud, all silvery and shiny in the afternoon sun. On any other day, at any other time, I might've thought that it looked kind of cool.

But I knew what that swarm was made of, and I knew what would happen if we couldn't escape it.

"Run faster!" I shouted to Mandy. *"Don't look back! Just run faster!"*

"Children!" Mr. Buggs screeched in my ear. *"How far are you from the Noteworthy Horn and Tuba Company?"*

"A . . . couple . . . of . . . blocks!" I huffed back

as I ran.

"You *must* make it! You *must* make it! There is a side entrance that is unlocked. Go there and get inside!"

Up ahead, I could see the big red building. The Noteworthy Horn and Tuba Company was built out of red bricks years and years ago. It didn't have a lot of windows, and I hardly ever saw anyone go in or come out.

"There it is!" Mandy cried. "There's the door he's talking about!"

Behind us, I could hear the buzzing of the swarm as it drew nearer. There were people on the street and in cars, and I wondered what would happen to them when the awful cloud of insects descended.

"I've got them!" Mr. Buggs suddenly exclaimed. "I've jammed my brother's frequency again! But there's still not much time left!"

We raced to the side of the building. I reached the door first and threw it open. Mandy darted inside, but I turned to see what had happened to the swarm. Other people on the street had spotted the silver cloud, and many of them stopped walking and peered up into the sky.

"Travis!" Mandy urged. *"Come on!"*

I turned and pulled the door closed. The room was dark, and I had no idea where we were or where to go.

"Mr. Buggs," I whispered. *"We're inside. Now what?"*

"There is a door on the other side of the room. It opens up into a hallway. Open it slowly. Other people might be around, and you don't want them to know that you are there."

I took a step in the darkness and bumped into Mandy.

"Sorry about that," I whispered. "Give me your hand."

"I can't see you," she said.

I reached out and found her arm, then I grabbed her hand.

"So we don't get lost," I said.

I walked slowly through the room. There was no light at all, and I didn't want to trip and fall over something.

I took a few steps, and then I bumped into a wall.

"Here we are," I whispered to Mandy. *"Help me find the door."*

We went back and forth over the wall for what seemed like forever.

"Here it is!" Mandy suddenly whispered in the darkness.

"Did you find the door?" Mr. Buggs's voice crackled in our ears.

"Mandy did," I replied.

"Good. Now . . . open it slowly. If you don't see anyone, go through the door and turn to your left. At the end of the hall will be a door that says 'private'. That's where you'll need to go."

"Ready Mandy?" I whispered.

"Anytime you are," she said softly.

I turned the knob, and pulled the door open. Light streamed through.

I opened the door just wide enough to peer out, then I poked my head through.

"It's clear!" I whispered to Mandy. *"Come on!"*

I opened the door wider and quickly stepped into the hall. Mandy followed.

But when I closed the door, I knew that our plan had been foiled.

There was a man behind the door!

When I'd opened it, he hid behind it . . . but when I closed it, he reached out and snapped the radios from our ears. He threw them to the ground and stomped on them. Then his strong, bony hands grasped our shoulders.

And I could tell right away that we were staring straight into the sinister face of Harry Buggs.

"Come in, come in!" Harry Buggs hissed with a nasty grin. *"I've been expecting you, children . . . ."*

29

Mandy and I were so shocked that we couldn't speak. I guess we'd never thought about getting caught by Harry Buggs himself.

He looked a lot like his brother, too. He had gray hair and a gray beard, and he wore glasses. But he didn't wear a white smock. Instead, he had on gray pants and a gray shirt with the words 'Noteworthy Horn and Tuba Company' emblazoned on the breast.

"Yes, the insects have eyes, children. I've known all along that you'd be coming. I'm not exactly sure what my brother has put you up to—but I can assure you, his plan will fail."

Harry Buggs gripped our shoulders tightly as

we began to walk down the hall.

"Interesting," he mused aloud. "My brother sends a couple of kids to try and stop me. That was very silly of him. I'm surprised that he underestimated me."

"You'll never get away with it," I said.

"Oh, I will, I will," Harry Buggs said. "I will show you how."

Just like Oliver Buggs had told us, at the end of the hall was a door with a big sign that said 'PRIVATE'. Harry Buggs opened it up and directed us through. Just beyond the door were steps, and he herded us down them.

"Yes, I'm a bit surprised with my brother," Harry Buggs continued. "All along, he's tried to figure out a way to stop me. I guess it's no secret who's got the brains in the family." He let out a laugh that sounded like a puking weasel.

Mandy was angry. She opened her mouth to say something, but I looked at her and mouthed the word 'no'. She understood, and didn't say anything. I didn't want to do or say anything that might make Harry Buggs upset.

We walked along a corridor with bare white

walls and white tile on the floor. Harry Buggs was wearing hard-heeled shoes, and his heavy steps echoed like thunder.

We came to another door. This one was locked. Harry Buggs took his hands from our shoulders and retrieved a set of keys from his pocket. They jangled as he inserted one into the lock.

Before he turned the knob, he looked at us with an eerie smile.

"I know my brother has told you that I have thousands of these insects," he said smugly. "Well, he is wrong. I don't have thousands."

He turned the knob, opened the door, and ushered us into a dark room. The door closed behind us, and we were in engulfed in darkness.

"No, not thousands," Harry Buggs said with a snicker. "Not thousands at all."

A light flicked on, and when I saw what was before us, I gasped in horror.

30

The room we were in was gigantic . . . like the size of Oliver Buggs's underground factory.

But that's not what was so scary.

It was the *insects.*

Harry Buggs was right . . . his brother had been wrong about how many insects he had. Harry didn't have just *thousands* of insects.

He had *millions* of them. Millions! They lined the floor, perfectly side by side, all facing the same direction. There were grasshoppers, bumblebees, mosquitos, and crickets. There were moths and beetles and dragonflies and locusts.

Millions of them.

"You see," Harry Buggs said, "I've been very,

very busy. And to think my brother wanted to use them as toys! Toys! Can you believe it?!"

"I think they'd make pretty cool toys," I said. "I'd buy one, if it didn't hurt anybody."

"Me too," Mandy said.

"You children don't understand how powerful these iron insects are . . . and how powerful I will be when I open the doors and unleash the swarm on the city. People will flee in horror!"

"You're a mean man," Mandy said. "You're mean and you're nasty and you won't get away with it!"

"Ah, you've been listening to Oliver too much. He probably has you convinced that he is the smarter one. Well, he's wrong. It is *I* who is the smartest. In fact, let us go to my laboratory. You two can watch as I program the insects and release them. Then, you can decide who is the smartest."

I wished that I still had my radio clipped to my ear. I probably wouldn't be able to talk to Oliver Buggs, but at least he might've been able to hear what was happening and could speak to me and give me instructions without his brother knowing about it.

We left the warehouse of insects and Harry Buggs closed the door behind us. Then he led us farther down the hall until we came to yet another door. This one was locked, too, and he unlocked it using one of the keys from his pocket. He pushed it open and waved us through. Then he pulled out another key and held it up.

"This door locks from the inside, too," he said, inserting the key into a lock on the door. "This is the only way out." He turned the key and removed it. "Just in case you get any ideas about leaving."

I looked around. The laboratory we were in really didn't look much like a laboratory. It looked more like a machine shop. There was a lot of heavy equipment and machinery that sat quietly.

"This is cool," I said, and Mandy stared at me. "You know," I continued, "I didn't think that Oliver was all that smart."

Mandy glared at me, and I glared back, hoping that she would catch on to what I was doing.

"Now you understand," Harry said. "My brother and his silly ideas of making toys. Ha! These insects aren't toys . . . they are weapons of terror."

"Yeah," I continued. "This is going to be cool. Can we watch?"

"Oh, certainly, certainly," Harry said. He sounded pleased, like someone finally realized he was the genius that he thought he was.

"Well, I'm not going to watch," Mandy said defiantly. She crossed her arms in disgust.

I looked at Harry Buggs. "Don't pay any attention to her," I said. "She's only a girl. She doesn't understand."

Mandy gasped and shot me a look of disbelief. She couldn't believe that I was treating her this way.

"Yes, she doesn't understand what true power is," Harry Buggs said.

"Like *us,*" I replied.

"Yes, yes *indeed!*" Harry exclaimed. "Come! It is time!"

"Travis Kramer, you're a rat fink!" Mandy

shouted. "I will never ever be your friend again! *EVER!*"

"Hey, fine with me," I sneered. "I've got a new friend that's smarter than you are." I turned. "Come on, Mr. Buggs. I want to see those insects take over the city."

Mandy remained by the door with her arms crossed while Harry Buggs and I walked across the lab and sat down at his desk. There was a large computer screen in front of us. Harry Buggs pressed a button and the computer whirred to life. The monitor blinked on, and I could see some of the buildings in downtown Elkhart.

"First, we'll need to release the swarm," Harry Buggs said, sitting down in a chair. There was another chair at another desk and I asked him if I could pull it up and sit down.

"By all means," he said without turning his attention from the computer screen. On the desk was a keyboard, and his fingers flew, tapping the letters and numbers.

I pulled the chair over and sat down next to him. As I sat, I turned to look at Mandy. She was still by the door, her arms crossed. When she saw me looking at her, she stuck her tongue out at me!

I hoped she would understand.

"Mr. Buggs," I said. "I think it would be really cool if you let me release the swarm," I said. "Please? That would be so awesome."

He looked at me, then smiled. "Why, of course, my friend. I can tell that you and I think alike. What we are about to do is a great thing."

He slid his chair over, and I slid mine closer to the keyboard.

"All you need to do," he said, "is to press this key here, and this one over here. That will activate the power in all of the insects."

"Like this?" I said. I pressed the keys. Instantly, a graphic flashed on the screen that read *POWER ACTIVATED.*

"Splendid!" Harry Buggs said. "Now . . . press this key, and this one over here to open the bay doors."

I did as I was told. Another graphic flashed on the computer screen. It read: *BAY DOORS ACTIVATED.*

"Wonderful!" Harry Buggs exclaimed. "Now . . . the final step. Now we will unleash the swarm!"

Harry Buggs showed me what keys to push.

"This is so exciting," I said. Then I turned around and looked at Mandy. "You don't know what you're missing," I said. "Get ready, Mandy. This is going to be cool!"

She crossed her arms tighter and said nothing.

I turned back and looked at the computer screen.

"Are we ready?" I asked.

"Anytime you are," he said, rubbing his hands together in anticipation. "I can't wait! I've waited for this moment for years!"

"This is going to be awesome!" I said.

And with that, I did something that Harry Buggs hadn't counted on.

31

In a flash I was on my feet. I spun.

"Mandy!" I shouted. *"Catch!"*

Mandy had a confused look on her face as the set of keys sailed through the air. While Harry Buggs had been showing me what to do, I was able to gently pull the keys out of his pocket!

"You little thief!" Harry screeched. He tried to grab me, but I ducked out of the way. Then I reached for the computer keyboard and pressed the 'enter' key.

"What are you doing, you ungrateful urchin?!?!" he exclaimed.

"Stopping you!" I said, and I darted away from him just as he tried to grab my arm.

Meanwhile, Mandy had succeeded in unlocking the door. I ran across the room while she held the door open.

"Fools!" Harry Buggs exclaimed. *"You think you've stopped me?!? Wrong!"*

I ignored him and kept running toward the open door. Mandy got out of my way as I leapt into the hall. Then I slammed the door shut.

"Give me the keys!" I ordered. Mandy handed them to me and I inserted them into the lock and gave them a twist. Then I pulled out the key and stuffed all of them into my pocket.

"He's not going anywhere," I said. "Let's get out of here!"

"I really thought that you had switched sides!" Mandy exclaimed. "Oooh! I was *so* mad at you!"

"I had to make you think that," I replied. "I knew that it would be our only chance."

"But what about the insects?" Mandy asked.

"When he wasn't watching, I slipped the diskette into the computer," I replied. "Harry Buggs is in for a big surprise. Come on! Let's get out of here!"

We ran down the hall, turned a corner, and ran up the stairs. I pulled the door open, and we were back in the main hall where Harry Buggs had first captured us. In no time at all we found the door that we had come through.

We were going to make it. Or, at least, we were going to make it out of the Noteworthy Horn and Tuba Company.

I opened the door. Mandy went through first, and I followed. Once again, we were shrouded in darkness, but it didn't take us long to find the side door that led outside.

I pushed it open and a warm breeze washed my face. Sunshine poured down as we stepped outside.

But something was wrong.

"Travis," Mandy asked. "Do . . . do you hear that?"

I nodded. Both of us looked up, only to see an enormous cloud of insects soaring up into the sky.

My plan had failed.

32

The weight of this disaster weighed heavy on my shoulders. I felt like the whole world had collapsed onto me.

Insects were soaring up into the sky, pouring higher and higher like smoke. We could hear the roar of their wings as they flew up into the air.

"I don't understand," I said. "I did just what Oliver Buggs told me. I put the diskette into the computer, just like he told me to do. I even selected it and pressed the 'enter' key!"

"We have to tell Mr. Buggs that we failed," Mandy said. "He'd know what to do!"

"Mandy," I began, "he's over a mile away! With the swarm of iron insects now released, we might not make it!"

"Well, it's the only thing we can do," Mandy said. "If we stay here, we can't do a thing. Maybe we have time to make it to Mr. Buggs's secret tunnel before the swarm attacks!"

I looked up at the swarm, then looked at Mandy. She was right, and I knew it. Maybe we *could* make it back to the tunnel. It still might be too late to do anything, but we had to try.

"Then let's go!" I exclaimed.

We stopped at the street and waited for several cars to pass. No one seemed to notice the growing swarm high in the sky.

We darted across the street and broke into a run.

"We can do it!" I said to Mandy as we raced along the shoulder. *"I know we can!"*

Actually, I really wasn't all that sure. I think I said those words to help convince myself that we had a chance.

Sweat began to pour down my cheek. The day was warm and the sun was still high in the sky. I didn't know what time it was but I was certain that it was getting late in the afternoon.

Half way there. Our shoes pounded the gravel, crunching like dry cereal. I glanced up behind me, only to see the swarm growing larger and larger. Mandy snapped her head around to get a look.

"We're going to make it!" she huffed. "We really are!"

Up ahead, I could see the small hill where the secret tunnel was. I ran faster, and so did Mandy.

But the roar of wings was getting closer. In my ears, I could hear the rumble of millions of beating wings. The swarm was getting closer, but I was too afraid to look. I knew Mandy was, too.

Finally, we reached the place in the field where we would cut through the tall grass and enter into the tunnel. We didn't have far to go.

But the roar of wings was louder, filling my ears like a freight train.

And when I glanced over my shoulder, what I saw made me realize that there was simply no way we were going to make it to the tunnel.

33

Just above us was a funnel cloud of insects, whirling and spinning like a tornado. In fact, that's just what it looked like: a tornado. High in the sky was an enormous cloud of insects . . . but coming right down was a spinning spout, twirling and whirling, made up of thousands of iron insects.

And it was headed right for us.

We bounded through the field, running faster than we've ever run in our lives. Sweat poured down my forehead and stung my eyes, but I hardly noticed it.

The buzzing roar grew so loud that it was unbearable. I wanted to reach up and cover my ears, but I wanted to keep my hand free in case one of the insects attacked.

Who am I kidding? I thought as the tall grass whipped at my legs. *I don't need to worry about one single insect . . . I need to worry about millions of them.*

The sun disappeared, and a shadow fell over the field. It looked really eerie. It was the middle of the day, but the swarm of iron insects had blocked the rays of the sun, and it looked like dusk, like the sun had just set.

I could see the entrance to the tunnel up ahead, and I started to think about what to do if we were able to make it there.

We'll dive into the tunnel, I thought. *We'll dive in and then we'll pull all of those branches and bushes over the entrance. A few might get through, but maybe we could fend them off.*

It was our only hope.

We ran, legs churning, bodies flying through the field. In the distance I could see the old factory. I knew that our bikes were still over there, near the front door. I wondered if we'd ever have a chance to ride them again.

Mandy screamed, and I turned just in time to

see her stumble. She tried to catch herself, but it was too late. She'd tripped on a rock, and plunged head first into the tall grass.

"Mandy!" I screamed. I stopped, turned, and raced back to help.

But there wouldn't be any time. Above us, the funnel of insects was fingering down, lower and lower, churning like a cyclone. Insects were only a few feet from us, and some of them were already buzzing by my head.

Mandy was still on the ground. She tried to get up, but I knew that it was already too late. The only thing I could do was try to protect her.

I dove down and landed on top of her in a heap, covering up as much of her body as I could.

Then I froze, and waited for the teeming swarm of insects to descend upon me.

34

The swarm of iron insects stormed above, and the buzzing roar was so close that it reverberated through my entire body. I could hear the insects, some of them swirling only a few inches from my ears. I knew that at any moment, one of them would attack, followed by another, then another and another.

The attack never came.

I waited and waited, frozen and unmoving, sheltering Mandy from the terrible onslaught.

But not a single insect even touched me.

Not one.

The longer I lay there, the more I began to think that maybe they *weren't* going to attack, after all.

With the roar of clapping wings still thundering in my ears, I slowly raised my head and looked up.

"Holy cow!" I whispered.

"What?" Mandy asked, her voice muffled by her hands. She was still face-down in the grass, her hands covering her eyes and cheeks for protection.

Above us, the insects still swarmed. But the finger that had streamed down like a threatening tornado was no longer coming directly at us! Instead, it had wound over the field . . . *straight into the entrance of Mr. Buggs's secret tunnel!*

"Mandy! You've got to see this!" I exclaimed.

"I can't!" she replied. "You're squishing me like a bug!"

"Well, you're the one that fell," I said. "There was nothing else I could do. That's the second time you've fallen today."

"Hey, I couldn't help it," was all she said.

I rolled to the side, but my eyes never left the incredible sight above us.

"Wow," Mandy whispered, after she had

rolled over and sat up. *"They weren't after us, after all."*

We watched as the swarm of insects above us dwindled down. After a few minutes, the last of them were gone.

We were safe . . . but I was suddenly shaken by yet another horrible thought.

"Oh no!" I cried. *"Mr. Buggs! The insects weren't after us! They were after Mr. Buggs!"*

Mandy's eyes grew wide, and her face grew pale. We looked over at the entrance to the tunnel where all of the insects had gone.

And we knew.

We knew that Mr. Buggs wouldn't have had a chance.

35

Maybe it was too late to help Mr. Buggs—

But maybe it wasn't.

"Through the factory!" I said, pointing to the dark building across the field. "We can go down using the elevator! It will be too dangerous to try and go through the tunnel with all of those insects. Harry Buggs might sic his insects on us next!"

I helped Mandy to her feet, and we ran across the field. In less than a minute we had arrived at the front door.

As we approached, the lock popped and the door opened all by itself. We raced through the main lobby and into the hall. The light popped on, and we ducked around cobwebs as we raced through the narrow corridors. It was kind of cool, zig-zagging through the building and having the lights turn on all by themselves.

Soon, we were at the elevator. The doors were already open, as if the elevator had expected us. We darted inside and the doors closed instantly. I reached out to press one of the buttons, but I stopped when the elevator began to descend all by itself. Oliver Buggs sure had thought of everything!

We plunged farther and farther into the earth, faster and faster. Then the elevator slowed. Once again, I was overcome by that strange feeling as the elevator came to a stop.

Without warning, the doors flew open.

Mandy screamed.

Even *I* screamed . . . and I don't scream very often. Right away, we realized we'd made a *big* mistake.

36

Everything in the factory—everything—was covered with iron insects.

Millions of them.

They were on the machines, they were on the floor. They covered the walls and hung from the ceiling. A few of them buzzed in the air.

Problem was, there was nowhere we could go. Right now, the only place where we didn't see any iron insects was right where we were . . . in the elevator.

"Well done!" a voice suddenly boomed out. Mr. Buggs appeared from around a piece of machinery. He walked carefully, pushing insects aside with his feet so he wouldn't crush any of them. He had a big smile on his face, and he spread his arms wide. "You did fantastic!" he exclaimed.

"We . . . we did?" I stammered. "I thought we screwed up royally."

He shook his head and approached the elevator.

"No, you did exactly what I asked you to do. I was worried, however, when I lost contact with you. I wasn't certain, but it sounded like you were captured by my brother."

"We were," Mandy said, bobbing her head. "As soon as we got inside. But Travis had a great plan, and he fooled him."

"It was perfect," Mr. Buggs said. "My brother didn't realize it, but as soon as he released the insects, I was able to take control of them from my computer. He didn't realize that you had reprogrammed his computer with that diskette until it was too late. I was able to control the entire swarm and bring them back here."

"So now what happens?" Mandy asked.

"Well, we have a lot of work to do. I'll be contacting some construction crews and have them completely renovate the Boogaloo Toy Company . . . the one that's above ground, that is. Hopefully, we can open up the old factory by next summer."

"Will we be able to buy remote control iron insects then?" I asked.

Mr. Buggs raised his eyebrows. "I have a better idea!" he exclaimed. He turned his head. "Katy!" he shouted. "Bring me one of the experimental giant insects!"

I heard a motorized whirring, followed by a shuffling sound. Then there was more whirring.

Katy Didd, Mr. Buggs's robot assistant, appeared in the aisle.

"Shoo!" she said to the insects on the floor. "Scoot! Shoo!" Insects crawled away from her.

She was carrying an insect—an iron insect—that was the size of a football. As she drew near, I could see that it was a big, shiny wasp. In her other hand she carried a small remote control box, and she handed both to Mr. Buggs.

"I think you two deserve this," he said. He stepped toward the elevator where we were standing and held out the giant silver wasp. "Go ahead," he said. "You'll have a lot of fun with it. Don't worry . . . it only flies. It can't sting you . . . not even accidentally."

I took the giant wasp from him, and Mandy took the remote control.

"Gosh, thanks!" I blurted out.

"Yeah, this is cool!" Mandy exclaimed.

"It is my gift to you. When the factory opens next spring, you'll have to stop by."

"We will!" Mandy and I promised at the same time.

"Well, then. I have lot of work to do. I hate to rush you off, but as you can see, I've got a lot of work ahead of me. Before you leave, however, I would like to ask one more thing of each of you. I would like to ask that you keep what you have seen a secret. I would like my inventions to be a complete surprise when the Boogaloo Toy Company opens again in the spring."

Darn, I thought. I wanted to tell all of my friends about what had happened.

"Okay," I said, and Mandy nodded.

"But what about your brother?" I asked.

"What's going to happen to him?"

"Oh, I wouldn't worry about Harry," Oliver Buggs said. I think he's not going to be causing anyone any trouble for a long, long time, thanks to you two. Good-bye, friends. I will see you in the spring."

"Good-bye," I said.

"See you later," said Mandy.

And with that, the elevator doors suddenly slid closed. The elevator started to rise. Our adventure was over.

Almost.

37

It didn't take us long to find our way through the factory and exit through the front doors. Our bicycles were on the ground, right where we'd left them.

"This thing is awesome," I said, gazing at the large robotic wasp that Mr. Buggs had given us. "Let's try it out."

I traded with Mandy. She took the iron wasp into her arms, and I took the remote control from her.

"This thing must weigh a ton!" she exclaimed. "I'll be amazed if it even flies!"

I fiddled with the nobs and dials. Suddenly, the wings of the wasp began to tremble. Mandy placed it on the ground.

I fiddled with another knob, and all at once the wings of the insect began to beat furiously. They moved so fast that they were only a blur. The noise of the wings sounded like electric hedge clippers.

"Just a little bit more," I said, turning one of the knobs.

"Travis! You're doing it! You're really doing it!"

The wasp lifted up, slowly, rising a few feet from the ground. As I gently turned a few of the other knobs on the remote, the hovering creature flew forward, then back, then to the side. Then it rose higher into the air.

"Let me try!" Mandy exclaimed. I handed her the remote and showed her which buttons controlled which movements.

"This is awesome," she said as the wasp sailed through the air. "This is even better than a remote control car!"

"Tons better," I agreed. "We're going to have a lot of fun with this!"

Mandy brought the iron wasp to a gentle

landing right at our feet. I carefully tucked the insect into my backpack, along with the remote control. Then we hopped on our bikes and headed for home.

As we rounded the street corner at the end of our block, I felt a huge sense of relief. What a day it had been!

"Do you think that there are any more of those insects around?" Mandy asked.

"I don't know," I replied. "I guess there could be a few. Mr. Buggs said that the ones we had found were insects that had malfunctioned, so there might be more."

We received a definite answer sooner than we thought. As we neared our homes, we were startled by the shrieking of a little boy. I hit the brakes and my bike skidded to a stop. Mandy did, too.

Between two houses we could see a small boy standing in a back yard. He was wearing only his swim trunks, and he was covering his head with his hands.

"No!" the frightened kid screamed. *"No!"*

Suddenly, we knew why he was so frightened.

High in the air, shining in the sun, an iron insect was heading right for him!

38

The insect was moving so fast that there was nothing we could do. We could only watch helplessly as the shiny attacker plunged out of the sky, faster and faster—

—and exploded right on top of the little kid's head!

The boy screamed in terror and ran.

"That wasn't an insect!" Mandy said in a rage. *"That was a water balloon!"*

Sure enough, we now could hear snickering coming from behind one of the houses.

And we knew right away who it was: Eddie Finkbinder and his goons.

"I can't believe he'd hit a little kid in the head with a water balloon!" she said.

"Come on," I said to Mandy. "If Eddie Finkbinder wants to pick on someone who is a lot smaller than he is, then let's give him a taste of his own medicine!"

"What do you mean?" Mandy asked.

I pointed to my backpack that hung from my handlebars.

"Let's see how the bully likes it when he's picked on by a giant flying iron insect," I said.

Mandy grinned. I have never seen a wider smile on her face.

We hopped off our bikes, pushed them into the yard, and stashed them behind some bushes so Eddie and his thugs wouldn't see them. I pulled the wasp from my backpack and handed it to Mandy. Then I pulled out the remote control.

"Ready?" I asked.

"Am I *ever!*" she exclaimed. "I keep thinking about that poor little kid!"

We crept along the side of the house, staying behind the bushes so we wouldn't be spotted. I peered around the corner and saw Eddie and his two friends filling up water balloons at a spigot. They were laughing and joking! They could have really hurt that little kid . . . yet they thought that what they had done was *funny!*

We backed up until we were far enough away that we wouldn't be spotted. Mandy placed the iron wasp in the grass, and I fiddled with the remote.

There was a buzzing sound. Its wings began to vibrate.

Then they began to flap.

Faster. Faster still.

I smiled and looked at Mandy.

"Go get'em, Travis," she growled.

"Oh, I'll get'em, all right," I snarled back.

We were about to give Eddie Finkbinder and his goons exactly what they had coming to them.

39

Guided by the remote control, the iron wasp rose up into the air. I let it hover in position while Mandy and I moved to a place where we could see better.

I peered around the corner, and Mandy leaned over my shoulder. Eddie and the goons were still filling up water balloons.

I turned and carefully guided the giant, remote-controlled wasp around the far side of the house. I wanted the flying insect to attack from the other direction, so Eddie and the other two kids wouldn't see us.

"Did you see that little kid go running off crying?" Eddie snickered. "That was great!"

"Grrrrrr," Mandy snarled over my shoulder. *"Eddie Finkbinder is nothing but a jerk."*

"Yeah, well, watch this," I said, and I lost sight of the wasp on the other side of the house. I made some adjustments to the remote, twisting the knobs and twirling the dials. Suddenly, I could see the wasp again, hovering above the roof.

This was going to be *spectacular.*

Eddie and his goons weren't even looking when the huge wasp swung right down in front of them.

"Whoah!!" one of the kids cried as the wasp whirled back up into the sky. The wasp had swooped down and up so fast that they didn't really know what was happening.

I turned another knob and the wasp rocketed down. All three of the kids were looking up, and when they saw the silver demon speeding toward them, they all dove to the ground.

"Ahhhhh!" Eddie screamed. He hit the ground and rolled. The other two kids had hit the ground. One was rolling as fast as he could, but he wasn't paying any attention where he was going, and he bonked his head on a tree trunk.

We could hear it thunk all the way across the yard!

"Eeeeeeyowww!!" he screamed. Over my shoulder, Mandy giggled and covered her mouth with her hands.

Meanwhile, I kept the wasp busy attacking. It swooped down on Eddie, then it dove down at the kid who'd bonked his noggin. It shot up into the air, then dove straight down at the other kid, who was so freaked out that he jumped the neighbor's fence and dove into a tiny wading pool.

"Every man for himself!" Eddie screamed. While he had the chance, he scooped up a handful of water balloons and fled . . . and he was coming our way! He was going to run right past us!

We ducked around the corner—but Mandy couldn't resist. When she heard his footsteps approaching, she stuck her foot out around the corner of the house.

Her timing was perfect. Eddie never even saw Mandy's leg, and he tripped.

His armload of water balloons flew out in front of him and he stumbled forward, trying to catch his balance—but he failed. He plunged face-first into the falling water balloons. They exploded in his face, drenching him from the waist up.

Mandy and I were hidden in the bushes, and I knew that if Eddie realized we were behind what was happening, he'd be furious. I managed a peek around the corner so I could see where the wasp was. Then I fiddled with a knob and brought the wasp sailing past the house and heading right for Eddie Finkbinder.

"Aaaahhhhh!" Eddie screamed. *"It's after me! It's after me!"* He leapt to his feet and bolted across the lawn, his arms flailing madly above his head. I chased him with the wasp all the way down to the end of the block before I brought the insect back to where we were.

"Travis," Mandy said, getting to her feet and emerging from the bushes, "that was awesome!" I climbed out from the bushes and stood. Mandy raised her hand and I slapped it, giving her a high-five.

"Oh, I'm sure we haven't seen the last of Eddie Finkbinder," I said. "But that sure got him back for being mean to that little kid."

And so, our strange adventure with iron insects came to an end. I was really glad that Mr. Buggs gave us that iron wasp to keep, and I couldn't wait for the Boogaloo Toy Company to open in the spring. It would be good to see Mr. Buggs again.

That night on the news, there were reports of a locust swarm that passed over the city. They interviewed a lot of people, but no one knew where the insects had gone.

I did, and so did Mandy. We just couldn't tell anybody that we knew.

By the time school started in the fall, I had become an expert at flying the iron wasp. But I kept it hidden most of the time, so people wouldn't see it and freak out. Sometimes Mandy and I would go to a park where no one was around and take turns flying the wasp. She got really good at it, too.

I wanted to tell all of my friends about what happened, but I remembered my promise to Mr. Buggs. Instead, I wrote a story about a kid who saves the world by using a remote controlled insect. It was a really cool story, and my teacher gave me an A+!

One day we were all given an assignment to study a state. Each one of us had to reach into a jar and pull out a slip of paper. On that paper was the name of a state. Our teacher gave us two weeks to finish our report.

I drew the state of Missouri. *What luck!* I thought. My cousin Amber lives in Kansas City, Missouri. I could call her and she could tell me all about her state!

So that's what I did. That night after dinner, I called Amber.

"Hey," I said, when I heard her voice. "Guess who?"

She paused a moment. "Travis? Is that you?"

"No, it's the tooth fairy," I said.

She laughed. "What have you been up to? I haven't talked to you since spring break!"

"You wouldn't believe me if I told you," I said, remembering the adventure that Mandy and I had with the iron insects. "In fact, I promised that I wouldn't tell anyone. Not until spring, anyway. How about you? What's been going on?"

There was a long pause.

"Amber?" I said. "Are you there?"

"Yeah, I'm here," she said. "It's just that . . . well . . . My friends and I just had a really freaky thing happen to us. In fact, the more that I think about it, the more I wonder if it was all just a nightmare."

"What?" I asked. "What happened?"

"It's creepy. It has to do with an old house not far from where we live."

"Tell me!" I insisted. "Is it a ghost story?"

"Worse," she said. "But it would take too long to tell you on the phone. I'll tell you what. I wrote it down on paper so I wouldn't ever forget it."

"You mean like a story?" I asked.

"Exactly," Amber replied. "I'll mail it to you, if you want to read it."

"Are you kidding?!?!" I replied. "Of course I would!"

Three days later, I came home from school and found a thick brown envelope in the mailbox. It was addressed to me, and it was from Amber.

I took the envelope inside, opened it, and began to read her story.

A story . . . that was *chilling* . . . .

next in the American Chillers series:

#10: MISSOURI MADHOUSE

turn the page to read a few chilling chapters!

My name is Amber DeBarre, and if you're reading this, there's a pretty good chance that you're a friend of mine.

Because I don't want just *anyone* reading about the things that happened to us. I wrote this down so I would always remember what happened to me . . . and to share what happened with good friends.

I live near Kansas City, Missouri. They call Missouri the 'show me' state. And while I can't really 'show you' what happened, I can *tell* you all about it.

And I will tell you right off: what you're about

to read isn't just an *ordinary* spooky story. In fact, if you frighten easily, you may not want to read this at all.

It all started one Friday night last summer. We live outside of the city where there are a lot of farms and old homes. My friend, Courtney Richards, lives about a mile south of us. She and her family just moved to the area, but we became best friends right away. She's eleven, just like me, and we're both in the same class at school.

On this particular evening, Courtney was coming to my house to spend the night. We switch every few weeks. I'll stay over at her house one time, and she'll stay at mine the next. We always have a lot of fun. We usually stay up late and watch scary movies on television.

Her parents dropped her off at seven o'clock. We ate popcorn and started to watch a scary movie in our basement. That's kind of our 'play' room. We have a big TV, a pool table, and a computer with a bunch of games. Whenever we have guests over, or when Courtney comes to spend the night, we hang out in the play room.

"This movie is *sooooo* boring," Courtney said

as she shoved a handful of popcorn into her mouth. "It's not even scary."

"I know," I said. "They sure don't make them like they used to. Remember the last one we saw?"

"You mean *'Revenge at Camp Creepy'?"*

"Yeah," I said with a shudder. "Now *that* was a scary movie!"

We watched for a few more minutes, but the movie just got worse.

"Geez," Courtney said. "This show is just *bad.* I want something that is *really* scary."

"I know of a place that's really scary," I said.

"You do? Really?" Courtney's eyes were wide. The television chattered on, but neither of us were paying any attention to it anymore.

"Yeah," I replied. "It's a house not too far from here. Have you ever heard of 'The Madhouse'?"

Courtney thought about it for a moment, then shook her head. "No, I haven't."

"It's not far from here. Nobody goes there anymore."

"Why?" she asked.

"Well . . . they just don't. They're afraid to."

"How about you?" Courtney asked. "Are you afraid to?"

I paused for a moment. I didn't want to tell Courtney the truth.

Because the truth was I was more than just afraid of the old place everyone called 'The Madhouse'.

I was horrified. But I just couldn't tell Courtney that.

"Oh, it scares *some* people," I said. "But not me."

"Take me there!" she said, her eyes brimming with excitement.

I looked at the clock on the wall. It was eight o'clock, and it wouldn't be getting dark for almost two hours.

"Well . . ." I said.

"Unless you're afraid, too," Courtney said.

"What?" I replied. "Me? Afraid? No way. We can go right now if you want."

"I want!" she said, jumping to her feet. Her blonde hair bounced around her shoulders. "A spooky old home! This is going to be *kew*-wool!"

Unfortunately, it wasn't going to be cool.

It was going to be terrifying.

The place we call 'The Madhouse' isn't far from where we live. It's at the end of an old dirt road. There are no other houses around it, and not many people have a reason to travel the road.

I told Courtney what I knew about the place as we walked.

"It's been there as long as I can remember," I said. "No one has lived there in a long, long time."

"So?" Courtney said. "There are lots of houses like that all over the place. Is it haunted?"

"Well, I don't know if you could say if it was haunted or not," I replied. "It looks really creepy, like a big face."

"The house has a face?!?!" Courtney said."

"Well, sort of," I replied. "When you see it, you'll know what I mean. And strange things have happened there."

"Like what?"

"Well, a long time ago, a boy used to live there with his family. But he never went outside."

"He stayed in the house?" Courtney asked.

I nodded. "That's what everyone says. They say that he never, ever left the house. Not once."

"What happened to him?" Courtney asked.

"Nobody knows," I replied. "But people say that he was really sad. They say that sometimes, if you look really close, you can still see him in the house. All you have to do is look into the windows."

"What do you see in the windows?" Courtney asked.

"Different people see different things, I guess," I replied. "But a lot of people say that they've seen a boy in the window. They say that he waves at them and wants them to come inside."

"That's weird," Courtney said.

"I know," I agreed.

"Have you ever seen anything in the windows?"

Should I tell her? I wondered. *Should I tell her what I saw last year?*

No.

I didn't want to lie to my friend . . . it's just that . . . well . . . I guess I'm not exactly sure *what* I saw.

"Let's just say that there is something weird going on at the house," I said. "I *know* there is."

Courtney shivered and giggled. "Kew-*wool!*" she said. "A real spookhouse! This will be a lot more fun than watching a dumb movie on television!"

"A *Madhouse,*" I corrected her. "Everyone calls it the Madhouse."

The evening air was crisp and cool. Both of us were wearing sweatshirts, and I was glad—because I noticed that as we got closer to the old house, the temperature seemed to drop. A cold wind breezed my cheeks.

The sun was still up, but it had dipped below the trees. We walked in the shadows of giant oaks and maples.

Up ahead, at the end of the street, the Madhouse came into view.

"There it is," I whispered.

"Wow," Courtney said. "It does look like a face."

And it did. The two-story home sat in the shade of the trees, and its windows were dark and forbidding, like cold, menacing eyes. The wood was old and gray like wrinkled skin. The front yard was overgrown with tall, sinewy grass.

"Somebody should fire the groundskeeper," Courtney said. "That guy hasn't done anything."

I laughed. Just the thought of a grounds-keeper working at the Madhouse seemed funny.

I felt a chill shiver through my body, and I wondered if it was just the wind. I didn't *feel* cold . . . but I shivered just the same. And as we drew closer and closer to the house, I began to feel more and more uneasy.

I had good reason to, as we were about to find out.

3

We stopped directly in front of the house, standing at the edge of the dirt road. Tall, uncut grass brushed our legs. A locust sang from the top of a tree, buzzing like a high-tension electrical wire.

Once again, that same chill swept through my body. Suddenly, I didn't want to be there. I didn't want to be there *at all.* I wanted to be home, in our play room, watching a scary movie on television, even if it *was* goofy. I wanted to turn and run . . . but I didn't.

"Wow," Courtney whispered. *"It looks even spookier from here."*

I pointed to the windows. "See how dark they

are?" I said. "Some people say that those windows are so black that you can't see any reflection."

"No!"

I bobbed my head. "Yep. They say that if you see anything at all, it's going to be something that is so weird that it will make you go mad."

"That's just plain silly," Courtney said. "I mean . . . the house looks creepy and all, but that just seems *silly.*"

"Hey, that's what they say," I replied.

"Well, then, let's go see," Courtney said.

All the time we had been walking, I was hoping that Courtney wouldn't ask to get close to the house. I was hoping that she would see it, get spooked, and that would be enough. I didn't think that she would actually want to get close to the house and look into the windows.

Another cold shiver slithered through my body as I looked at the house. Tall grass swayed gently. A soft breeze purred through the trees.

"Well?" Courtney said.

I wanted to turn and run. I wanted to go home. I didn't want to be here.

And so, when I heard myself saying 'okay', I knew right away that I was making a big mistake.

We both were.

Without another word, we began to walk through the waist-high grass.

Toward the Madhouse.

"Wait."

I spoke the word as I grasped Courtney's hand. We both stopped walking, and she turned to me.

"What is it?" Courtney asked.

"I . . . I just . . . oh, I don't know," I said. "It's silly."

"What?" Courtney asked. "What's silly?"

"I just feel . . . *weird,* I guess."

"You're right," Courtney said with a smile. She gave my hand a squeeze and let it go. "You *do* feel weird. Come on."

I took a breath, and we continued walking through the grass. The sun was dropping fast, but a few thin blades of light still knifed through the thick trees. It would be dark soon.

More locusts droned from the trees, and their buzzing drowned out all other sounds. The singing insects were so loud that I couldn't even hear our feet crunch through the tall grass.

"What do you think we'll see?" Courtney asked. She sounded excited, without a hint of fear in her voice at all.

I, however, knew better.

"Oh, I don't know," I replied, my eyes bouncing from one dark window to the next. "Probably nothing."

We were almost to the house. I was glad that it wasn't dark yet.

"See anything?" Courtney asked.

I shook my head. "Nope."

"We probably have to be closer," she said. "I think it would be cool to see something in the windows. Wouldn't that be spooky?"

"Yeah," I replied with a nervous laugh.

We stopped. Four old, rickety steps led up to the porch. The wood was gray and worn. I reached out and touched the railing and it felt gritty and dry beneath my fingers.

Courtney and I craned our necks to see into the windows.

"They sure are dark," she said. I didn't say anything, and we just stood there for a moment, looking up at the old home that loomed over us.

The Madhouse.

"Come on," I said after a few moments. "Let's go home before it gets dark."

"Just a minute," Courtney said, and she placed her right foot on the first step. Then she raised her left to the next. I stayed right where I was.

She looked back at me. "You're not coming?" she asked.

"I'm going to stay right here," I said.

"Fine with me," she replied. Then she took two more steps and was on the porch. Cautiously, she walked toward a window.

"I don't see anything," she said. "The window is really dark."

"Can you see inside?" I asked.

Courtney shook her head. "No. It's too dark. I can see my own reflection, though. I guess that means that I'm not a vampire."

I giggled. We watched a movie about vampires once, and we found out that vampires don't have a reflection in mirrors or glass.

Of course, vampires don't *really* exist, but we thought it was kind of funny anyway.

"There are some more windows on the side of the house," I said. "We can go look there."

Courtney shrugged. "Okay," she said. "But I don't see why they call this place The Madhouse. It doesn't look any different than any other old house."

She turned and stepped off the porch, and we waded through the tall grass to the side of the house. Here, the final rays of sun streamed through the trees, and I breathed a sigh of relief. It wasn't as dark on this side of the house.

We approached a window and stared at it. We could see our reflections clearly, but nothing else.

Courtney raised her hands, placed her thumbs in her ears, and wiggled her fingers. She stared at her own reflection in the window.

"Look!" she exclaimed, raising her eyebrows. "I'm a monster! Booga, booga!"

I laughed. She looked really silly.

"Booga, booga!" she said again, wiggling her fingers faster. I laughed at her reflection in the window. "See?" she said. "The Madhouse has made me crazy! Booga, booga!"

She stuck her tongue out and wagged it back and forth while she wiggled her fingers. I laughed so hard that tears came to my eyes.

"Booga, booga!" Courtney giggled, rolling her eyes. "Booga–"

Suddenly, Courtney stopped moving. She stopped speaking.

She had a strange look on her face, and she slowly lowered her hands. She squinted and peered into the window.

Her curious expression turned to one of shock. Her head jerked back. I looked into the window.

Our faces reflected in the dark glass, but now we could see something else. At first it was fuzzy and murky, but as we watched, the image cleared.

Suddenly, I noticed that the forest around us had become very still and quiet. No locusts buzzed, no breeze whispered through the trees.

That familiar chill swept through me again,

only stronger this time. My whole body tensed. I gasped. Courtney's mouth opened to scream, but no sound came out.

She had a good reason to be horrified. I did, too.

There was *another* face in the window.

The face of a boy.

"Hey guys! What's up?"

I jumped and gasped at the same time. Courtney spun around.

"Scott!" I scolded. "You scared us to death!"

He looked at me, then at Courtney. "You look pretty alive to me," he said.

Scott Palmer has been my friend for a long time. We're in the same grade, and we used to be in the same class. He lives a few houses away from us. He's the same height as me, and his brown hair is almost identical to the color of mine . . . except his is a lot shorter.

"I didn't mean to sneak up on you," he said. "I stopped by your house and your mom said that you had gone for a walk down here."

"Yeah, well, you surprised us all right," Courtney said. She'd met Scott a few times, but they didn't know each other real well.

"Checking out the Madhouse, huh?" he said, peering into the window. "See anything?"

"No," I replied, shaking my head.

"Nothing at all," Courtney said.

"Well, a lot of people have," Scott said. "My dad says there are a lot of weird things that happen at this house."

"I want to see something!" Courtney whined. "I really do!"

"You need to stare into the window for a long time," Scott said. "You can't just look into a window and look away. You really have to concentrate."

"Scott," I said with a cautious tone of warning in my voice. "I don't think that's a good idea."

"All you have to do is just focus on one place in the glass," Scott continued, ignoring me. "Go ahead, Courtney. Try it."

"Scott!" I pleaded. "Don't—"

"Oh, come on, Amber," he said. "Don't be

such a chicken."

"So, all I have to do is stare into the window?" Courtney asked. She glanced at her reflection in the glass, then turned to Scott.

"Yeah," he said. "But you really need to concentrate. Give it a try."

Courtney turned back toward the window. "Okay," she said.

I grabbed Scott by the arm and pulled. He walked with me to the front of the house, leaving Courtney standing before the window. We were far enough away so she couldn't hear us, but we stayed in a spot where we could see her.

"You shouldn't have told her that!" I hissed.

"What's the big deal, Amber?" he hissed back.

"The 'big deal' is that something is going on at this house," I said. *"Nobody knows what, but there is something going on here!"*

"Yeah, well, nobody has ever been hurt, have they?"

I glanced over at Courtney. She was a few feet away from the house, gazing into the window.

"No," I replied. *"Not yet."*

"Then quit your worrying," Scott said. *"Besides*

. . . she probably won't see anything, anyway."

We watched Courtney for a moment. She continued to gaze into the window.

Finally, I walked back to her. "Come on, Court," I said. "Let's go home."

Courtney didn't say anything.

"Hey," I said, waving my hand in front of her face. "Come on. We don't have to watch that dumb scary movie. We can watch something else."

But Courtney didn't even blink. She didn't move or speak.

"Courtney?" I asked. "Courtney?"

Still, there was no response from her.

Suddenly, her eyes grew wide. I turned my head to look into the window, but I only saw my own reflection and Courtney's horrified expression glaring back at me.

Her mouth opened. Slowly, she raised her arm and pointed at the window.

And screamed.

FUN FACTS ABOUT INDIANA:

State Capitol: Indianapolis

State Stone: Indiana Limestone

State Song: "On the Banks of Wabash"

State Bird: Cardinal

State Nickname: Hoosier State

State Tree: Tulip tree

State Motto: "The Crossroads of America"

State Flower: Peony

The total area of Indiana is 36,420 square miles!

INTERESTING INDIANA TRIVIA!

☞ **The original plans of Jeffersonville City, Indiana plans were originally drafted by Thomas Jefferson.**

☞ **The first automatic headlight dimmer was developed in Anderson, Indiana in 1952.**

☞ **Singer Frank Sinatra debuted in Indianapolis at the Lyric Theater with the Tommy Dorsey Orchestra on February 2, 1940.**

☞ **The name, "Indiana" was coined by Congress in 1800 which means, "the land of the Indians."**

☞ **Indiana became a state on December 11th, 1816.**

Also by Johnathan Rand:

GHOST IN THE GRAVEYARD

About the author

Johnathan Rand is the author of the best-selling **'Chillers'** series, now with over 1,000,000 copies in print. In addition to the **'Chillers'** series, Rand is also the author of **'Ghost in the Graveyard',** a collection of thrilling, original short stories featuring *The Adventure Club.* (And don't forget to check out **www.ghostinthegraveyard.com** and read an **entire story** from 'Ghost in the Graveyard' ***FREE!***) When Mr. Rand and his wife are not traveling to schools and book signings, they live in a small town in northern lower Michigan with their two dogs, Abby and Salty. He still writes all of his books in the wee hours of the morning, and still submits all manuscripts by mail. He is currently working on his newest series, entitled **'American Chillers'**. His popular website features hundreds of photographs, stories, and art work. Visit:

www.americanchillers.com

For information on personal appearances, motivational speaking engagements, or book signings, write to:

AudioCraft Publishing, Inc.
PO Box 281
Topinabee Island, MI 49791

or call
(231) 238-0297

About the cover art: This unique cover was designed and created by Michigan artists Darrin Brege and Mark Thompson.

Darrin Brege works as an animator by day, and is now applying his talents on the internet, creating various web sites and flash animations. He attended animation school in southern California in the early nineties, and over the years has created original characters and animations for Warner Bros (Space Jam), for Hasbro (Tonka Joe Multimedia line), Universal Pictures (Bullwinkle and Fractured Fairy Tales CD Roms), and Disney. Besides art, he and his wife Karen are improv performers featured weekly at Mark Ridley's Comedy Castle over the last eight years. Improvisational comedy has provided the groundwork for a successful voice over career as well. Darrin has dozens of characters and impersonations in his portfolio. Darrin and Karen have a son named Mick.

Mark Thompson has been a professional illustrator for 25 years. He has applied his talents with toy companies Hasbro and Mattel, along with creating art for automobile companies. His work has been seen from San Diego Seaworld to Kmart stores, as well as the Detroit Tigers and the renowned 'Screams' ice-cream parlor in Hell, Michigan. Mark currently is designing holiday crafts for a local company, as well as doing website design and digital art from his home studio. He loves sci-fi and monster art, and also collects comics for a hobby. He has two boys of his own, and they're BIG Chiller Fans!

All AudioCraft books are proudly printed, bound, and manufactured in the United States of America, utilizing American resources, labor, and materials.

USA